Six and Silver

Illustrated by
MARGARET HORDER

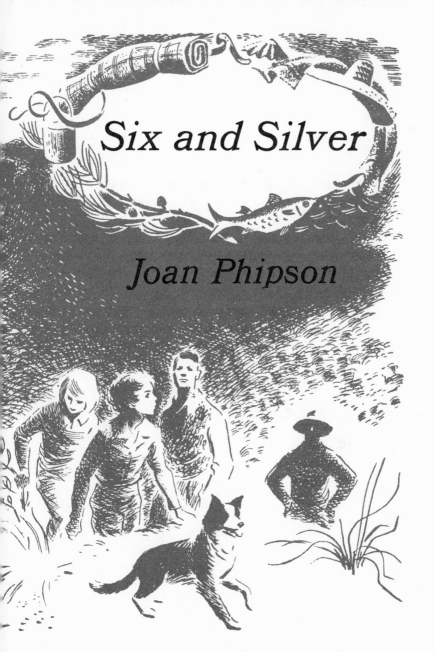

Six and Silver

Joan Phipson

HARCOURT BRACE JOVANOVICH, INC.
NEW YORK

First American edition, 1971

Originally published in Australia by Angus and Robertson in 1954.

ISBN 0—15—275330—3

Library of Congress Catalog Card Number: 70—152696

Printed in the United States of America

A B C D E F G H I J

CONTENTS

CHAPTER ONE

Strangers on the Beach

"*T*here they are again," said Jack as he climbed over the back of the battered utility. "Anyone would think they owned the beach." He grabbed his towel, jumped down, and skipped as the hot sand burned his feet.

His father, stepping more deliberately from the driving seat, glanced across the sand to where the big beach umbrella made a splash of color against the surf and then turned to his son, the merest twinkle in his eyes.

"Perhaps they do," he said. "At any rate, we can't imagine that three weeks' rent of a cottage gives us any rights on the beach." He slammed the door, threw his towel over his shoulder, and started off toward the water.

"Possibly not, but they don't have to be darned ostentatious about their beastly beach umbrella and their negroid suntans," answered Jack, whose own back still showed the blotched red and white marks of a painful sunburn.

There was a thud on the sand beside him, and a compact girl of thirteen with short, straight fair hair, a cheerful mouth, and a sunburned nose landed on all fours. She picked herself up, looked around eagerly, and gave an exclamation of satisfaction as she saw the beach umbrella. "Oh, good. I'm glad they're here again. They're such fun to watch. They're so *good* at everything."

Jack glanced down at his sister and snorted. "The trouble with you is you've no critical faculty."

"I'm not jealous, if that's what you mean," she answered.

Jack looked down at her and grinned suddenly. "Very well, Miss Steadman. Come along." He turned toward the surf. On the far corner of the truck's tailboard, the rear end of a small boy slid rapidly out of sight.

"Where's Billy?" asked Jack.

"He's off after Father," said Pat, pointing to where the small boy scuttled across the sand like a rabbit. "Come on. I can hardly wait for my morning dump."

Jack looked at her curiously. "Do you always get dumped?"

"Mostly. But I'm learning. I don't swallow nearly so much water as I used to. Haven't you noticed?"

"It's hard to tell," said Jack, "when all I can ever see of you is a couple of legs sticking out of the froth."

"I know," said Pat with a sigh. "I always seem to be upside down."

They were approaching the beach umbrella and the group of drowsy figures that lay beneath it. Jack eyed it distastefully. "Don't you mind?" he asked. "In front of those?"

Pat looked at him in surprise. "No," she said. "Of course I don't. Do you?"

He didn't answer immediately, but she caught a quick,

embarrassed frown and found herself trotting to keep up with him. "Oh," she gasped when she could get her breath, "so that's why you haven't been trying to get shoots lately. Oh, Jack, you are funny! And I thought it was so kind of you to spend all that time teaching Billy to swim." She burst into a peal of laughter, and under the beach umbrella one of the sleepy heads was raised to watch them pass.

But Jack still frowned and seemed to have lost interest in the conversation. They walked on in silence.

Away to their right the long crescent of the beach, the color of old ivory, lay dazzling in the morning sun; and at the far end, nursed in the crook of encircling hills and protected from the sea by a strong outcrop of rocks, clustered the houses of the seaside town, its brief water-front bristling with Norfolk Island pines. Near them on the left the beach ended in a flurry of rock, seaweed, and spray. This morning the sea was very blue, its long lace edging of surf lazy and inviting as fold on fold of waves came smoothly to the shore.

As they walked down to where their father sat waiting for them on the edge of the water and where their small brother was already digging like a puppy in the wet sand, Pat and Jack looked an oddly assorted pair to be brother and sister. Jack, broad-shouldered and thickset for his sixteen years, with a head of thick, dark hair, and Pat, small and smoothly rounded, with childishly supple limbs and wide, friendly eyes, seemed to have little in common except their noticeable and distressing lack of suntan. But, perhaps because they were so different and in spite of the three years between them, they understood each other very well. Only within the last few days, since they had begun to notice that particular beach umbrella and those it shaded, had they found themselves out of agreement.

Mr. Steadman looked up as they dropped down on the sand beside him. "Well," he asked with commendable gravity, "did you manage to pass them without mishap?"

"I didn't hear any personal remarks, if that's what you mean," said Jack. "I can't say I noticed them particularly."

"I did try to," said Pat, squeezing a worm of white cream onto her nose. "But Jack was in such a hurry to get past that I didn't have a chance. But I do believe the older one has *another* new outfit on." She smeared the cream over her face with a lavish hand. "How lovely it must be to have a dry bathing suit for every swim."

Jack made a noise that sounded like "Sissies" and rolled over to let the sun do its worst on his back.

Mr. Steadman tipped his oil-spotted felt hat farther forward and smiled at the white mask of his daughter's face. "Never mind," he said. "You're sure to have a better view before long. Their morning sun-worship must be nearly over. I must say," he went on thoughtfully, "I like seeing them in the surf. They're so competent." As this was the highest praise Mr. Steadman ever allowed himself for anyone, it reduced his children temporarily to silence.

Pat finished anointing her shoulders and legs and passed the tube to Jack. "You'd better do your back," she said. "Remember how sore you were last night."

"It's right, thanks," he answered. "It'll be brown soon now."

"Not if you let it peel off all the time," said Pat. "I'll do it then." The tube was poised over his back, the cream squelching out, when Pat, glancing down the sloping sand toward the water, suddenly dropped the tube and sprang up.

"Oh, heavens!" she gasped. "Quick, Jack. He's over again." She ran down to where the last boiling flurry of a wave was casting the upended form of her small brother into the shallows. When she caught him and set him right side up, he blinked wetly, coughed, and opened his mouth to let forth a satisfying roar of protest. But the frothing approach of the next wave caught his eye, the roar changed to a shout of joy, and he turned and flung himself upon it.

"Oh, dear," said Pat in dismay. "He'll be drowned for a certainty. It seemed such a good thing when he stopped being frightened of the surf, and now I wish he hadn't."

"Got to risk it," said Jack, wading in after them. "You wouldn't want him to be a coward."

"Yes, I would," said Pat firmly. "A live mouse is always better than a dead lion."

Jack, horrified by such sentiments, was about to reprove her when Mr. Steadman, his felt hat discarded, waded through the surf toward them.

"I'll look after Billy," he said. "Go and have your swim."

"Oh, thank you, Father," said Pat with relief. "Come on, Jack. I'm really going to get a shoot today." She turned to face the breakers. With one doubtful look at the distant beach umbrella, Jack followed her out.

For some time they battled hard and happily. Jack, a better swimmer than Pat, and stronger, succeeded in riding several waves almost to the beach. But Pat, to her annoyance, for she was trying very hard, could make no progress except, inadvertently, upside down, or being bowled violently over and over along the bottom. But the water, glittering and sparkling in the hot morning sun, was too pleasant to leave, and time after time she climbed to her feet, pushed the lank strands of hair out of her eyes, and waded back to try again.

Jack, too, was enjoying himself. After the long summer months at home in the crackling dry air of the Northwest, the very wetness of the sea was a never-failing delight. They forgot time, they forgot their father and Billy, they even forgot the direful proximity of the big beach umbrella.

So it was with a slight shock of surprise that Pat, jumping high over a purposeful breaker, saw a brown body shoot past her on its crest and ride it with no apparent effort until it reached the beach. She looked around then and saw with delight that several heads were bobbing up and down beyond her out by the farthest line of breakers. The beach umbrella had been deserted, and its owners had taken to the water. As she watched, a big wave picked them up and bore them gloriously in toward her, and at the same time she saw Jack, not quite so far out, battling valiantly to pick up the same curling green wave. But he was too late, and as he swam forward, the wave curved, poised, and crashed down on top of him. The brown figures on its crest came sweeping on toward the shallows, but of Jack there was no sign. She waited anxiously for him to appear again, but it was not until the others were standing up on the edge of the water that she saw him rise, disheveled and red-faced, from the suds of foam that the wave had left behind it. He coughed, gasped, and shook the water from his head, and then saw the beach-umbrella party splashing toward him, making for the deep water again. Pat saw a frown like thunder settle on his face, and he turned and left the water to fling himself on the sand beside their towels, his face toward the shore.

She smiled to herself and turned back to the surf. Her eyes were on the bobbing heads farther out. As far as she could make out, there were six of them: three girls and three bronzed and streamlined young men. The girls wore white bathing caps and brief but gaily colored suits. One girl, she thought, looked rather smaller and perhaps younger than the others, but to her inexperienced eye they all seemed enormously proficient. They must, she thought, spend their lives on the beach to acquire that rich, even tan and that superb prowess in the surf. One after another, or sometimes all together, they swept past her, borne by breakers that would have dumped her in a minute. And as they waded back again, they shouted to one another and laughed and splashed with infectious high spirits. It did not seem possible that these were the people who had lain supine beneath the beach umbrella a little while before.

After a time she heard her father call and saw him signal to her to come in. She plunged once more under a wave for luck and then made for the beach. Mr. Steadman was rubbing himself briskly with his towel, and Billy was raising his usual wail at being dragged from the water.

"Better go up now," said Mr. Steadman. "Your mother will be wanting to get down to the beach herself after lunch."

Jack climbed to his feet, cast one glowering look at the surfers, and started for the utility. Pat dried herself, swung the wailing Billy onto her back, and cantered after him. Mr. Steadman came more soberly behind them.

In a very few minutes the utility drew up under the

trees at the back of the small cottage they had rented for the holidays. Mrs. Steadman waited for them at the back door. She was a large, brisk-looking person with Pat's wide, friendly mouth, wavy fair hair just beginning to turn gray, and kind, shrewd eyes.

"Just in time," she said when the engine was turned off. "Dinner on the grass today. I grilled the steak on the outside fire to save mess. Run and get your clothes on."

Soon they were all sitting on the springy buffalo grass under the trees with their plates in front of them. Pat, like the others, ate ravenously. Her skin still tingled pleasantly from the salt water, and she felt, as she always did after a swim, that her mind, like her body, had been washed clean by the sea.

"Well," asked Mrs. Steadman. "What's the news today?"

Pat looked up, her fork poised. "They were there again, Mother; six of them. And they were so *heavenly* in the water." She sighed dreamily, and the piece of steak dropped off her fork.

"We can't decide," said Mr. Steadman thoughtfully, "whether to admire them deeply for their ability in the water, or to detest their presumption in lying about on our piece of beach." He glanced for a second at Jack, who was devouring his steak as if it were to be his last meal on earth.

Mrs. Steadman laughed. "I expect they are just like us, really; enjoying their holidays while they can. It would be nice for Pat and Jack if they could get to know them, especially as they seem to be the only other people always on the beach."

"Oh, wouldn't it?" said Pat, as if this delightful possibility had never occurred to her. But Jack put down his knife and fork and said firmly to his mother, "It wouldn't be at all nice. I can't see that we have anything in common with them. For goodness' sake, Mother, don't go smiling at them or asking how their lumbago is, the way you do."

"I do not think they are sufferers," said Mr. Steadman decidedly into his plate.

"Very well, then," replied Mrs. Steadman. "I won't, if you think it better not." Only Pat caught the glimmer of a smile in her eyes. "But I must tell you that I have found out where they live."

"What?" said Jack in alarm.

"Have you, Mother? Oh, where?" asked Pat eagerly.

"That modern little white house on the hill with the plate-glass windows. The one we liked so much," said Mrs. Steadman. "The baker told me."

"I'm glad," said Pat. "I did hope they'd live in a nice place like that. It makes it all just right."

"Right for what?" asked Jack.

"I don't know. Just right. I couldn't have borne them to live in one of those nasty, peeling little wooden houses by the lake."

"Do them good if they did," said Jack as he deftly twitched another piece of steak off the gridiron.

"Oh, well," said Mrs. Steadman peaceably, "let's forget about them now. What are we going to do this afternoon? Whatever it is, I'm taking my sketchbook with me."

For the rest of the meal they discussed their afternoon's activities and their mother's deplorable habit of cumbering herself with sketchbook and pencils whenever they all set out together.

This was the first time the Steadmans had left their property in the northwest of New South Wales and come south to spend a holiday by the sea. In the early days when Pat and Jack were small, they had felt they could not afford the expense of such a wholesale evacuation. Later, when Mr. Steadman's brother John had come to join them on the property and was starting his cattle stud, Mr. Steadman had found he could not get away at such a busy time of year. Then Billy arrived, and it was not until he was big enough to travel easily that holidays at the seaside were considered seriously. To Pat and Billy it was proving a time of unclouded joy. They loved the beach, the sea, the climbs over rocks and dunes, and the timeless days when meals turned up, not by the clock, but when it suited Mrs. Steadman's fancy to serve them. They loved—particularly Billy—the novelty of living with parents who had apparently forgotten the tiresome necessity of bringing them up and who, for once, seemed content to let them enjoy themselves in their own peculiar ways and in their own time. Here, except for warnings about traffic on the roads, bluebottle stings, and going out too deep, there were no rules and no penalties. It was heaven.

For Jack it was a little different. At sixteen he felt the need for independence and self-expression; and here, though there was much that he enjoyed, he was, to a certain extent, denied both. At home he was accustomed to driving any or all of the motor vehicles, from the family car to the crawler tractor, and was already proving a useful driver at times when they were shorthanded. But here he was never allowed to take the wheel in case a lurking policeman should pounce on him because he was under age. Also, at home he could hold his own with most of the men in almost all of their occupations. Here, every long-legged, suntanned child could surf, dive, or handle a boat better than he could. He was out of his element and sure that it was as obvious to everyone else as it was to himself. But for all this, when he forgot about it, he enjoyed himself.

In the afternoon they went for a walk along the beach. Officially it was a walk, but Mr. Steadman took his fishing rod and Mrs. Steadman her sketchbook.

There had been a time when Mrs. Steadman had planned a career for herself as an artist and had studied at the Technical College. She was on the way to success when she married and had then found that running a home in the country and bringing up children did not leave time for a career as well. Now she sketched only for pleasure when the opportunity offered and did not regret her lost career.

So when they reached the end of the beach under the lee of the headland, Mrs. Steadman sat down on the sand and opened her sketchbook. Mr. Steadman walked out along the rocks with his rod, Billy skirmishing in his wake among the rock pools, and Pat and Jack made for the tip of the big headland. After a stiff climb they rounded the point. The wind hit them, salt-laden and boisterous, and the cliff plateau they had climbed ceased in a jumbled fall of huge upended boulders, the sandstone grained in fluid, sweeping lines of darker brown. Beyond the tumbled rocks curved another beach, remote and solitary far below them. At its far end another headland shouldered out to sea. To their right, a long way down, the sea stretched for mile on endless mile until it met the sky. Except for one or two tiny distant steamers, there was no sign of life anywhere. For a few minutes they looked in silence. Then Pat said, "It was worth climbing up to see, wasn't it?"

Jack nodded. "It's very *big*, isn't it? But now I want to

see what there is round that next headland. We seem to have been cheated by this one."

Pat turned to him and smiled. "I can tell you if you really want to know."

"Can you?" he said in surprise. "I didn't know you'd ever been up there."

"I haven't. But I know just the same."

"Do you?" said Jack. "Tell me, then."

Pat's smile widened. "On the other side you will find another beach—and then another headland."

Jack grinned. "Smart, aren't you?" he said, catching her by the elbows and shaking her. "I suppose I knew it too, but it doesn't stop me wanting to see with my own eyes."

"I expect it's the same feeling that makes explorers keep wanting to explore," said Pat when she regained her footing. "Well, go on—explore. I'll sit here and watch you."

But Jack shook his head. "I'd like to someday, but we'd better be getting back. The sun's pretty low already." He glanced upward with the countryman's eye for the time of day.

They found Mr. Steadman reeling in his line when they returned. He was wet and contented, but there were no fish. Billy was even wetter, having used his own method of fishing in the rock pools.

"Look!" he shrieked when he saw them. He held out his hand, and they saw a small and remarkably dead fish.

"It was dead when he caught it," murmured Mr. Steadman. "But it would never do to say so."

Mrs. Steadman had spent a satisfactory afternoon and showed them a lively drawing of Billy catching his fish.

"Looks as if he just fell on it," said Jack.

"That's his technique," explained Mrs. Steadman.

The sun sank as they walked home, and the first hint of dusk turned the sea from the cheerful blue of the afternoon to a dull, mysterious green that seemed to enfold the secret and teeming life beneath the water. And now the evening fishermen came out from their cottages and seaside shacks and took up their stand, one by one, along the darkening beach.

It was almost night when they reached the cottage, and Mrs. Steadman bustled into the kitchen to make cocoa and boil eggs. In a short time they were all sitting around the big table in the living room, Billy in his robe, sleek and washed. Already his face began to assume the angelic look of all small children prepared for bed. On the table beside him stood a small, woolly lamb. It had once, with its genuine lamb's wool and beady eyes, been a life-

like animal, but now one of its eyes had fallen out, its nose was rubbed off, and there were bare patches on its head and legs. It was, to Billy, who was so far behind Pat and Jack that he was almost in the position of being an only child, a companion, confidant, and guide; and when he felt acutely his lack of years, it was Pinkie, the invincible, the all-wise, who lifted him from his inferior position. Pinkie had, in fact, been for so long one of the family that no one now thought it worth while to comment on his presence at the supper table. Billy regarded him for a moment and then said, "Pinkie says he catches whales when he goes fishing."

"I dare say," replied Jack. "We know all we want to about Pinkie. I suppose he catches them with a bent pin."

"Pinkie," answered Billy with an air of finality, ignoring the flippant suggestion, "makes the sun rise up." He turned his attention to toast and honey.

Supper over, Billy and Pinkie retired to bed. When the washing-up was done, the others settled down in the living room, Mrs. Steadman with her knitting, their father with the paper, and Pat and Jack with a pack of cards beside the table. The big glass door onto the veranda stood wide open, and from beyond the trees that surrounded the house, they could hear the continuous boom of the surf, punctuated from time to time by the staccato slap of a wave. A multitude of insects drifted in and hummed around the light.

CHAPTER TWO

Trial and Error

*T*he next day an incident occurred that filled
Pat with delight and Jack with dismay. They were down
on the beach as usual, this time with Mrs. Steadman as
well, so that Pat and Jack, with no obligation to watch
Billy, had gone straight into the surf. Once again the
beach umbrella stood poised on the sand, but this time its
owners were already in the water. In consideration of
Jack's feelings the Steadmans took to the surf a little way
down the beach. They had not been in very long before
Pat noticed one of the girls leave the group and make her
way toward them. Jack, after one glance, dived under a
wave and went farther out, but Pat waited until she
came up. At close quarters Pat could see that she was
quite young. With the white cap on, it was hard to tell
exactly, but Pat guessed she must be fairly near her own
age. She had a vivid, delicate face and a pair of dark,
intelligent eyes. She smiled as she approached, and Pat
noticed that her teeth were very white and straight.

"Hello," she said. "You're the country people in that
brown cottage below us, aren't you?"

"Yes," said Pat, smiling back.

The girl nodded. "I thought so. That's why I came over. I thought you probably didn't realize. I don't want to be interfering or anything."

"Oh, no," said Pat, a little mystified. "Of course not."

"You're swimming in a runout here—a channel, you know."

"Oh," said Pat. "Are we? Does it matter? Oughtn't we to be?"

"It does matter rather," said the girl candidly. "You *could* get washed out, especially if you're not very strong swimmers."

"I'm not," said Pat quickly. "I'm hopeless."

"I know," said the girl with a friendly grin. "I saw you. But you do try, don't you? I can't say I'd care to be dumped as often in a morning as you are."

Pat laughed. "This is our first time at the sea, you know."

The girl's eyes opened in surprise. "Is it really? No wonder you can't pick a runout." She glanced out to where Jack was being kept busy diving under the big waves. "I think I'd call your brother in if I were you. Why don't you come up and swim near us? There are so few people down here generally, and we always pick the safest bit of surf."

Pat's blue eyes brightened even more. "Oh, thank you. I *should* like it. It's so difficult when you don't know anything."

"Of course it is. Well, I'd better be getting back. I'm Tess, by the way. All those others except Mary, my sister, are just friends staying with us. Good-bye, then. See you later." She gave Pat a warm smile and went quickly back up the beach.

Pat turned and went out until she could make Jack hear. He came in at her call and walked up to her suspiciously.

"Well, what's it all about?" he asked.

Pat told him and suggested, a little nervously, that they should follow Tess's advice and move up to where her party were swimming.

But Jack refused flatly. "No, thanks. I've had enough for today anyway. I'm going to lie on the sand for a bit. You go up if you want to." He turned and left the surf, and Pat stood with the foam bubbling around her feet, looking first at him and then at the group farther up. Tess had joined them again now and was out with the farthest of them, her head bobbing like a little white cork as she waited for a shoot. Pat wanted very much to go, but she couldn't quite find the courage to join them on her own. She was sure that Tess would not mind, but the others were all more grown up and might find her a nuisance. She gave a small sigh and followed Jack up the beach.

Shortly afterward they went back to the cottage. At the dinner table Mrs. Steadman said, "It was nice of the child to come over specially to tell you."

"It was the right thing to do," said Mr. Steadman, "if they thought these two were in any danger. But, naturally, deeply mortifying at the same time."

"More like darned cheek," said Jack.

Pat, knowing Jack's sensitive pride, was sorry for him. "I think it was me she was worrying about more than Jack. She said she noticed I couldn't swim."

"Did she, indeed?" said Jack, bristling.

"Yes," said Pat. "And it's quite true, of course. I'm sure she felt Jack could look after himself." Her blatant untruth had its reward in a brief smile from Jack. "I'm only sorry if she thought we didn't *want* to go over to them when she asked us specially."

"And nothing, of course, could be further from the truth," said her maddening father.

Later in the day Pat was walking a little distance behind the rest of the family along the shore of the small lake that spread itself among the tea trees and the scrub behind the beach. She was wondering rather anxiously what she should say to Tess when a voice called her. That is to say, from somewhere quite nearby she heard, "Oh, hey! I say!"

She stopped, and a slim figure in washed-out blue shorts and a striped cotton pullover slid off the landing stage of one of the boat sheds that lined that side of the lake. She didn't recognize it at first. The short, dark, curly hair looked very different from the white bathing cap she had seen before. But after a second or two she recognized Tess.

"Hello," she said a little shyly.

"Sorry I had to bawl at you in that vulgar way," said Tess. "But I don't know your name, you know."

"It's Pat—Patricia Steadman, really," said Pat. Then, taking the bull by the horns, she went on quickly, "You must have thought us rather rude not to come over this morning when you asked us. I did so want to, but Jack" —she floundered and then went on—"Jack said he'd finished his swim anyway. But we were awfully grateful to you for telling us."

"That's all right," said Tess. "I know exactly. Boys do hate to be *told*, don't they? But we thought you ought to know."

"Oh, yes," said Pat, disconcerted for the moment. Then

her face widened into a smile. "They do," she said with feeling.

Tess laughed. "Well, never mind. But you'll come and surf with us when you want to, won't you? To tell you the truth, I'm a bit of an outsider just now. All the others are Mary's friends, and they will treat me like the kid sister. It can be frightfully tiresome."

"I'd love to," said Pat. "You're sure they won't think me in the way?"

"Good heavens, no," said Tess in surprise. "Why on earth should they? But I might as well warn you they'll probably treat you like a kid sister, too."

"I shouldn't mind that at all," said Pat. "I suppose—I suppose you come here quite a lot, don't you? We always think you all look as if you lived on the beach."

"Sort of barnacle-encrusted, I expect," said Tess.

"Oh, no," said Pat, horrified. "I mean, you're all so brown and swim so well, and you have all the right things, and so many bathing suits and everything."

Tess looked at her with amusement. "That'll be Mary. She's always buying them, like some people collect postage stamps. The place up there"—she nodded toward the hill behind them—"is peppered with Mary's cast-off outfits. It's handy in a way. I never have to buy any myself—just take a tuck in Mary's old ones. But we do sort of live down here. I mean we've had the cottage for years, and we come down whenever we can."

"Are you from the city, then?" asked Pat.

"Yes. We live in Sydney. But we only get brown down here, you know. It never quite seems to wear off. But tell me, do we look as brown as all that? Like natives, I mean?"

Pat blushed, remembering Jack's blistering remarks.

"No," she said, shaking her head violently. "Oh, no! Only—only professional."

"That's good," said Tess. "We never worry, you know, but some of them—some of Mary's friends—go to no end of trouble. You'd be surprised. They come down here for weekends, and they're so busy getting brown, they can never do anything but flop about in the sun. Silly, I call it. This lot aren't too bad, though. In fact, rather nice, really." She pointed, and Pat noticed for the first time two little sailboats out on the glittering surface of the lake.

"Are they your boats?" asked Pat.

"Yes. They're such fun. Have you ever sailed?" Pat shook her head. "We'll take you out one day."

As they watched, the little boats turned and battled along side by side until they reached the point. Then they turned again slowly, the sails swung out to catch the wind, and bit by bit they gathered speed until they disappeared out of sight.

"Come on," said Tess. "Let's go along to where we can see them."

But Pat suddenly remembered her family. "I'd love to," she said. "But I'll have to go, or they'll think I'm lost."

"Right you are," said Tess. "But come and surf with us tomorrow if you can." With a quick parting smile she turned, and Pat watched her racing up the shore of the lake, her long legs flying and the short curls bouncing as she ran.

The next morning Mr. Steadman said uncompromisingly, "You'll both have to swim with the others today. We can't afford to run any risks."

Jack lifted his head quickly to protest, but Mr. Steadman interrupted him. "I'm sorry if you don't like it. You can wait and swim when they've finished if you like, but now that they've taken the trouble to warn you, I'm afraid you'll have to take their advice. I didn't realize there was any danger, or I would always have made sure it was safe before you went in." He was adamant, and Jack had to give in with the best grace he could.

When they went down to the beach, the umbrella was already in position. Underneath it six people were lying, apparently unconscious, spread out star-fashion, their heads in the shade and the rest of them in the full blaze of the sun. As the Steadmans passed, Tess, who must have been more wide awake than she looked, jumped up and ran across to them.

"Hello, Pat," she shouted. "I've been hoping you'd turn up soon."

Pat greeted her with a smile and started to introduce her to the rest of the family, remembering, too late, that she did not know her surname.

"How silly of me not to have told you," said Tess. "Our name's Moorland."

Mr. Steadman, liking what he saw, nodded pleasantly. Jack said, "How do you do," with rather aloof politeness, and Billy gazed at her with frank curiosity.

"Pinkie has swum to New Zealand," he informed her when his curiosity was satisfied.

For a moment Tess's eyes opened wide. Then she replied gravely, "Has he really? How splendid! I had a white mouse once that made a noise like an alarm clock whenever I was going to get the hiccups."

Billy regarded her with dawning admiration. Then he uttered a yell of joy and made for the surf. They watched him fling himself, face first, into the bubbles, and then Tess said, "Were you thinking of going in at once?"

"I don't think we'd decided," replied Pat, with an inquiring glance at Jack.

"For myself," said Mr. Steadman, "I propose to spend the major part of the morning ruminating on the sand. I shall guard Billy."

"I'm going to sunbake for a bit," said Jack. He was at last beginning to acquire an even tan, and he was rather proud of it.

"Well, I thought that if you weren't all plunging in immediately," said Tess, "it might be a good idea if Pat and I went over to the lake for a while and did a bit of swimming practice. It would help you in the surf. That's if you don't mind," she added quickly.

"Oh, no, I'd love it," said Pat.

So they made their way back to the still water of the lake. And here, for half an hour or so, Tess did her best to instruct Pat in the proper movements and the correct way to breathe. Pat, determined to be a credit to her teacher, struggled manfully. Time after time she tried to synchronize arms, legs, and breath. Time after time she breathed out when she should have breathed in, forgot to kick, or splashed along, her arms working like windmills until Tess would shout, "No! *Don't* dog-paddle. This way."

And once again she would demonstrate, cutting through the water with an ease and speed that filled Pat with admiration and envy.

Tess turned out to be a hard taskmaster. Nothing would satisfy her but the best, and Pat, who was always slow to learn, began to feel she would never grasp the trick of it.

At last, when in her efforts to obey she had taken a deep breath with her head under the water and come up red in the face and choking, Tess gave a shriek of despair, clapped her hands to her head, and waded out. When Pat reached her, mortified and apologetic, she was sitting in the sand, her arms around her knees. To Pat's surprise, for she had thought Tess had quite lost patience with her, Tess patted the sand.

"Take a seat," she said. "You must be nearly drowned."

"I'm awfully sorry," said Pat, sitting down. "I was always silly at learning things. But I should so like to be able to swim properly."

"And I never have enough patience," said Tess. "But don't worry. You'll be all right. I've often noticed that people who learn slowly are the best in the end. You'll probably find that you do much better tomorrow."

"Do you really think so?" said Pat humbly.

Tess nodded. "The darkest moment before the dawn, you know. And you were darned near extinguished that time, weren't you?"

For a while they sat in companionable silence. The lake twinkled in the morning sun, and from time to time they saw a small splash as a fish jumped.

"Mullet," said Tess. "They'd make good bait for your father."

"Would they?" said Pat. "Father would so like to catch a fish before we go home."

"When do you have to go?" asked Tess.

"In about a fortnight," said Pat. "We couldn't get the cottage for all the holidays."

"What a shame," said Tess sympathetically. "As a matter of fact, we have to go back about then, too. Mother told some noisome cousins of ours they could have our cottage for the last week. I do think being generous has some ghastly drawbacks, don't you?"

"Sometimes," said Pat.

"And there you are, you see. We could have let you have it. What a shame," said Tess, disgusted.

"But then you still wouldn't have had it," said Pat logically.

"That's true," said Tess. "But at least those appalling cousins wouldn't either. They always tramp porridge into the floor. I can't think why."

"Do they really?" said Pat in amazement.

"Well, that's what it looks like," said Tess. "We've never actually had the stuff analyzed."

"I don't think we ever do that," said Pat seriously.

"No," said Tess thoughtfully. "Your family don't look the porridge-tramping sort. I don't believe it's a country habit."

"Oh, I hope not," said Pat. "Though I couldn't say for sure with Billy. How did you know we were from the country?"

"Oh, I don't know," said Tess. "You can always tell. People look sort of open-airy."

"We thought you all looked terribly grown up and clever," said Pat.

For a while they discussed this interesting topic, and then a shadow fell across them and a voice from behind said, "You seem to be having a lovely gossip over here all by yourselves. We're going for a swim now, Tess. Are you coming?"

Pat looked up to see a tall girl with a pleasant, tranquil face and wide dark eyes like Tess's but with a soft expression that Tess's lacked.

"Hello, Mary," said Tess, looking up. "This is Pat Steadman. My sister, Mary," she explained to Pat.

"Hello," said Mary with a friendly smile.

"I've been teaching her to swim," said Tess.

"I know," said Mary. "We saw. We wondered how long it would be before you drowned her. I'm very glad to see you're still conscious."

"I'm not very good, I'm afraid," said Pat.

"It wouldn't matter how good you were—she could still drown you. She's never satisfied, you know."

"Rot," said Tess succinctly.

"But you've one consolation," went on Mary calmly. "If you manage to survive, she'll have you swimming like a veteran before you've finished."

"She's been very good and patient," said Pat loyally.

"Of course I have," said Tess, jumping up. "For an elder sister, Mary, you talk an awful lot of piffle. Come on, Pat, let's go and have a surf." She started off at full speed for the breakers.

Pat, feeling it was not quite right to run off and desert the owner of so many ravishing bathing suits, politely regulated her pace to Mary's.

"She's a terrible girl," said Mary as she watched her young sister streak across the sand. "But I'll tell you one thing—but never let her know I told you; it would make her far too swelled-headed—she swims better than any of us. And I'm not so bad myself," she added thoughtfully.

As they approached the surf, they saw that all the others were already in the water. A little farther along the beach, Jack still lay sunning himself beside his father.

"Shall we go and ask your brother to join us?" asked Mary. "It would be much better, really. I had a nasty feeling I should be having to go and rescue him yesterday. I always feel I should, you know, and I do so hate it."

"Yes—thank you," said Pat dubiously. And they altered their course accordingly.

But she need not have worried. Mary, when she had been introduced to Mr. Steadman and Jack, said at once, "We're going in now. How about coming with us? I always like a lot of people round me in the surf—sharks and things, you know," she added vaguely.

Jack capitulated at once to this tactful invitation and got up. "Yes, of course," he said graciously.

Contrary to his forebodings, the morning passed happily for all of them. Under Tess's tuition Pat did better than she had ever done before, no one attempted to be patronizing, and at the end Jack's confidence was wonderfully restored when he achieved the best shoot of his brief surfing career. So that when as they were leaving the water Mary came up to Jack and asked if he would go sailing with them in the afternoon, he accepted with more pleasure than Pat had thought possible.

She went with him down to the Moorlands' boat shed at three o'clock, and they found Mary, Tess, and two of their friends already there.

"The other two went in to do some shopping," said Tess. "I'm so glad you could come and help us out. It's such a nice breeze, it's a pity to miss it."

The two boats were drawn up on the bank, and the Moorlands and their friends were wading about doing obscure things, it seemed to Pat, with ropes and sails and an assortment of long poles, some of which miraculously resolved themselves into masts as they watched. Mary and one of the young men were preparing the larger boat, and Tess, with another whose name, Pat gathered from Tess's frequently hurled instructions, was Mac, was busy with the smaller one. In a short time, with the mast up, the sail flapping, and a number of ropes dangling in a very untidy way, the little boat was ready.

"All right," said Mary, peering over the bow of her own boat. "Off you go, Tess. We'll have a trial run up the lake and back, and then we'll have a race."

"Right," said Tess. "We'll see you later. Hop in, Mac. I'll push off." Pat saw the sail bulge and fill, and the little boat glided smoothly out into the open water. Before long Mary straightened up and called out to her partner, "Are we right now, Bill?"

"I think so," he answered. "I'll swing her round while you assemble your crew."

"That means you," Mary explained to Jack as she waded ashore. "You hop in when Bill says, and go and sit down amidships, will you? We'll tell you what to do as we go on."

Jack, looking puzzled but interested, stepped aboard and sat down hurriedly where he had been told. Mary and Bill pushed her out and jumped in neatly as she took the water. Pat settled herself comfortably against the boat-shed wall and watched them move up the lake after Tess. Very soon both boats had rounded the point and were out of sight.

For a time nothing moved on the lake. There was no sign of the little boats; even the ripples of their wake had crossed the water and lapped themselves away against the farther shore. Then two or three shags rose lazily from over the trees at the point, disturbed by the passing of the boats on the other side, and flapped away to sea— gaunt black birds that showed touches of white as they flew. A little while later there was a rush of wings, and some twenty or thirty black swans flew over in formation, banked, and wheeled around over the lake again, and Pat guessed that the little boats had reached the marshy head of the lake where the swans lived. After that it did not seem long before she saw the white triangles of the sails appearing around the point, and soon they were back, sails flapping, just off shore from where she sat. They waved to her, and Tess shouted, "We're going to race now. Watch us."

They were side by side when their sails filled simultaneously, and they started off. They both swung wide to avoid a long black stick that rose out of the lake about halfway across. A sudden gust of wind came just as they rounded it and heeled both boats over. Pat saw Jack make a sudden movement, and the bigger boat altered course quickly. She thought she heard Tess call out something about rocks, and then the boat jerked unexpectedly, the mast shivered, the sail swung out and caught the wind, and she saw Jack on his feet bending over something amidships. The boat swayed, trembled, and turned over.

Pat jumped to her feet as she saw its crew tumble into the water. The sail settled gently like a tablecloth on the lake, and the boat came to rest, its keel visible just above the surface.

Tess sailed her little boat over, turned it into the wind, and stood by, observing with interest the wreck of her opponent. Pat heard her call out, "Are you all right?" And Mary's voice from somewhere among the tackle at the stern replying, "Do we *look* all right?" and ending with a burst of laughter.

"What have you done with Jack?" Tess shouted back, and Pat was dismayed to realize that she could see only two heads in the water. But now she noticed that the sail, at first so tranquil, was behaving in the oddest manner.

A round nob would form, like a boil, in one part of it, only to subside and rise again in another, and over the whole area of sail there was some sort of violent agitation. It appeared to have taken on a life of its own.

"Look under the sail," shouted Tess again. And Mary, after a brief, "Oh, my heavens!" and an irrepressible giggle, dived out of sight. At the same moment Bill, at the bow, duck-dived with one swift kick. The antics of the sail became less, the boil disappeared, and Mary and Bill between them shepherded a very waterlogged Jack to the side of the boat. He was gasping a little and his face was red, but more, Pat thought, with anger than distress. They spoke to him, and she saw him nod; and then Mary could contain herself no longer, and peal after peal of laughter rose from the capsized boat.

After a few minutes Tess called out irritably, "Do you think it would be a good idea to fix the boat up?"

Mary's laughter subsided. She wiped her eyes on a sodden sleeve and shook her dripping head. "Yes," she said with a gulp. "But you must admit it was funny."

After that they worked on the boat and by degrees got it to the shore, righted it, tipped the water out, and spread the sail on the grass to dry. Tess and Mac sailed in and helped them.

When it was finished, Tess regarded the shipwrecked mariners dispassionately and remarked, "If I were you, I'd go home and change my clothes. You all look frightful."

"Oh, well," said Mary philosophically as they tramped, dripping, up the road. "Better luck next time. I'm sorry we tipped you out on your first sail, Jack. But you can't say it wasn't exciting."

They reached the crossroads, and as they parted, Jack

uttered a gruff, "It was my fault, I'm afraid. I'm sorry."

That evening when the Steadmans were at supper, Jack, who was forced to explain the state of his clothes, gave his parents an account of the afternoon. He was suffering from an acute sense of grievance.

"They call every darned thing by something else's name. And, 'Hang on to the sheet,' Mary screams, and I make a grab at the sail. 'No, not the sail,' she says, and a great baulk of timber comes along and cracks me over the ear, and I sit down again. 'I meant that rope there,' she says when my head's singing like a beehive. Then I'm told to pull something else, and I pull it, and the boat tips over and I hang onto something else to stop myself going into the water and she screams again, 'Look out, you'll have us over.' Then all of a sudden we hit the bottom, and Bill shouts, 'Pull up the centerboard, Jack.' And naturally I start pulling planks out of the bottom of the boat. It seems a darned silly thing to do, but I'm supposing they know best, till Mary's suddenly at me again: 'Hey, don't pull the boat to pieces; pull up the centerboard, that big iron thing below.' So I start hunting round for a slab of iron, and it turns out to be something underneath the boat all the time. I ask you! So by the time they start talking plain English and I find the thing I'm supposed to be pulling, the blessed boat's all over the place and that Mary, who I will say never loses the use of her tongue, calls out, 'We're over, chaps.' But by that time I could have told her that, and there we are, all in the lake, and the next thing I know is I'm trying to fight my way up through the sail. When I'm darned near drowned, somebody grabs my arm and nearly dislocates my shoulder, and someone else twists my collar and chokes out what bit of wind I had left. So I come to the surface, pretty near dead, and the first thing I see is the lovely Mary laughing fit to kill herself. I suppose if she'd throttled the life clean out of me, she'd be laughing yet." He stopped, and dead silence settled on the company. Mr. Steadman had his hand over his eyes, and his shoulders shook a little.

After a spellbound moment Billy spoke. "Pinkie once tipped over an aircraft carrier. He rescued the captain from the water with one hoof."

CHAPTER THREE

An Experience for Jack

*A*fter this ill-starred episode, relations between the Moorlands and the Steadmans were a little aloof for a few days. Tess and Pat still saw a lot of one another, the swimming lessons still went on, and Jack continued to surf with them. But his manner, which had seemed to be on the verge of thawing, was distant, and when they asked him a second time to go sailing, he found that he had more pressing engagements.

And then, at the very tail end of the holidays, another more serious episode occurred that made him announce, loudly and frequently, that henceforth he would take his holidays at Alice Springs and the rest of the family could go where they pleased.

For some days they had noticed that every morning the beach became more empty as, one by one, the few families they had begun to recognize by sight went back to their homes. Then, one morning, there were only two figures under the Moorlands' beach umbrella, and Tess told Pat that their friends had had to go back, too. The beach now appeared quite deserted, and Jack, gathering confidence as the regular inhabitants thinned out, said to Pat one day that he thought he would try a dive or two from the springboard at the edge of the lake. Pat knew that he had practiced diving in the bore dams at home and was pleased that he should be keen enough to try here.

"Oh yes, Jack," she said. "That would be a good idea. I'd love to come and watch—if you don't mind," she added diffidently.

"Of course not. I don't mind you a bit," he said kindly.

"Shall we go tomorrow morning instead of surfing?" she asked. But he shook his head.

"Too many people about. We'll go after dinner, and we might have the beach to ourselves for a while."

Pat knew he was thinking of the Moorlands. "All right," she said. "After dinner tomorrow."

It so happened that the Steadmans' dinner that day consisted of roast beef and apple pie—a filling meal. And when Pat and Jack set off for the lake afterward, they both felt rather more inclined to sleep than to swim.

"Isn't it a bit soon after dinner?" Pat asked him once.

"Perhaps it is a little," said Jack. "We can lie on the sand for a while first if you like."

But when they reached the end of the lake where it lapped against the piled-up sand of the beach, they found Mary and Tess stretched out half-asleep. Across the water opposite them where the sand dunes rose up more sharply from the lake, the springboard waited invitingly. Jack would have liked to avoid them—would have liked, in fact, to have postponed his diving until they had gone elsewhere, but he felt still less inclined to remain beside them on the sand.

"Well, what shall we do now?" he hissed at Pat, as if it were her fault.

"If we lie on the sand, we'll have to lie with them," said Pat. "It would be too rude if we went and lay down farther on."

"That settles it, then," said Jack. "We'll go straight round to the springboard."

"Are you sure it's all right?" asked Pat doubtfully.

"It'll have to be," said Jack. "We can hardly turn round and go back." So they marched on, and as they approached, Tess looked up in surprise.

"Hello, where are you two going? I thought you were having lunch."

"We've had it," said Pat. "Jack's going to do some diving." She was proud to be able to mention Jack's accomplishment, but Jack scowled at her.

"A bit soon to swim after a meal, isn't it?" asked Mary, rolling her head over on her arm and opening one eye sleepily. "I hope you didn't eat too much."

"Oh, I'm all right," answered Jack a little brusquely. "That sort of thing never worries me."

"Well, go steady," said Tess. "You never can tell."

"I'll be right, thanks," said Jack, and walked on.

"Have you had your dinner?" asked Pat curiously.

Tess shook her head sadly. "Unfortunately, no. And I'm as hungry as a hunter. Mary says she hasn't had her sleep out, so we have to wait till she has. There's no one at home but us, so it doesn't really matter. But I'll be able to watch Jack now, and that'll pass the time—even if he doesn't like an audience," she added mischievously.

"I'd better go and catch up with him," said Pat as she watched him striding around the head of the lake. "I'm only going to watch, but I said I'd go with him."

"Well, just see that he goes carefully," said Tess more seriously than usual. "It really is a risk, you know."

"I know," said Pat unhappily, and she ran off after Jack.

When they reached the diving board, Jack threw down his towel and turned to Pat. "What are you going to do?" he asked.

"Just sit here and watch you," said Pat.

"A bit boring for you, isn't it?" he asked. "Why not have a go, too?"

"Oh, no thank you, Jack," said Pat, alarmed. "I'd much rather watch you."

He grinned at her. "Very well, then, I hope I can give you something worth watching." As he looked up, his eye caught the two prone figures on the sand around the bend of the lake. "But I wish those two weren't there. I'll bet they both dive like seals—and know it."

"I think they're both asleep again by now," said Pat. "I'm sure Mary is, anyway."

"Good," said Jack, and stepped onto the springboard. "Now watch me and tell me what I do wrong."

He walked to the end of the board, tested its spring once or twice, and then dived. It was quite a good dive, and he hit the water without too much splash. After a couple of seconds he came to the surface, took a gulp of air, and swam to the shore. "How was that?" he asked Pat as he climbed out.

"It looked very nice," said Pat. "You might have gone a little farther forward, perhaps."

"Right," he said. "I'll have another go. The water's pretty cold just here." He wiped his face with his hands, and Pat noticed that his nails were blue. He was shivering slightly.

"Do you think it would be better if you waited a little while?" she asked as tactfully as she could. But he shook his head.

"No. It's just the first shock. I'll get used to it in a minute." He climbed up onto the board again and walked to the end. "I'll try and get farther out this time." He poised, tensed himself, and dived again. This time he shot forward, hit the water with a smack, and disappeared in a shower of spray. A ring of bubbles spread where he had entered the water. Pat looked for him to reappear a little farther out, but for nearly a minute nothing broke the surface. She jumped to her feet and then drew a deep breath as she saw him come up almost in the same place where he went in. But to her surprise it was his shoulder that appeared first; when his head came up, she noticed that his teeth were clenched and his eyes looked strange and wild. He shouted something that she could not catch, and before she had time to answer, he disappeared again. In sudden terror she called out, "Jack!" And then remembering, shouted with all her might, "Tess! Tess, come quick!"

To her relief she saw that Tess was already running around the edge of the lake. Mary followed a little way behind.

By the time they reached her, Jack had come up once more, but this time he uttered no more than a strangled gasp before he disappeared again. Tess halted only long enough to shout at her, "He's got a cramp," before she dived in from the bank.

"You stay there," said Mary, and dived in after her.

To Pat, watching helplessly on the edge, it seemed an age before they reached the spot where Jack had appeared last. They both duck-dived with scarcely a ripple, and when they came up, she saw with relief that Jack was between them. He appeared to be quite unable to help himself, but they got him to the shore at last and with Pat's help they pulled him out and laid him facedown on the sand. They put his towel under his head, and Tess got down on her knees and started to pump the water out. But he could not lie still, and as Tess tried to work, he twisted and turned as if he were in pain. Mary, standing over him and watching carefully, said at last, "I don't think that's necessary, Tess. He seems to be breathing all right. We'd better get busy on his muscles. The cramp's still got him."

She got down on her knees as well and started to massage him energetically. Tess did the same, and Pat,

once she realized what was needed, helped them. After a while he grew quieter, his twisting and turning ceased, and soon, to Pat's relief, they heard his voice, a little hoarse, but quite strong.

"I'm all right now, thanks."

Mary and Tess sat back on their haunches, panting. Tess wiped her arm across her face.

"Whew!" she said. "And on an empty stomach, too."

"Good for the figure," said Mary cheerfully. Then, as Jack rolled over and sat up, "How do you feel now?"

He looked about vaguely. "All right, I think. What happened?"

"You got a cramp," said Mary. "That ghastly pain was a cramp. I know; I've had it myself. Beastly."

"So that was it?" said Jack. "I thought it was something I'd hit in the water."

"What you hit *was* the water," explained Tess. "You hit it with your tum the second time—if you'll forgive my saying so."

"And being straight after lunch," added Mary. "But if you feel all right, I think we can pronounce you cured now. Can you get up?"

"Yes," he said at once, and scrambled to his feet. But he swayed for a minute, and Pat ran to take his arm.

"I don't think you'd better try diving any more for today," said Mary, taking him firmly by the other elbow. "We'll walk up with you. We were going up, anyway. Come on, Tess."

They took him as far as the Steadmans' gate, and by the time they reached it, his color had come back.

"There you are," said Tess. "A nice cup of tea now, and you'll be a new man."

With his hand on the gate he turned to them. "Thanks very much for dragging me out and—and fixing me up," he said gruffly, and made his way up the path.

Mary touched Pat quickly on the arm. "Don't look so worried," she said. "He'll be quite all right now."

"Thank you both very much," Pat said breathlessly, and ran up the path after Jack.

The next morning, to Jack's annoyance, Mrs. Steadman would not let him go down to the beach. He protested that he felt fine, that he never felt better in his life, that a cramp was something anybody was likely to get at any time, and anyway it was all over now. Mrs. Steadman smiled, sympathized, agreed patiently with everything he said, but remained firm. He had not slept well in the night, and they had heard him coughing more than once. And no matter how he felt, he was pale and looked tired.

"But there are only three more days left, Mother," he argued. "I might just as well lie about on the sand as up here."

But she shook her head. "I'd like you to stay here, Jack," she said quietly. And he stayed.

He was more silent than usual at breakfast and up till the time the others left for the beach. For once, when Tess's or Mary's name was mentioned, he had no biting comments to offer. Pat hoped that he had forgotten his grievance. Mrs. Steadman must have felt the same, for she said to him once, "It was a mercy those two girls happened to be there yesterday. I don't like to think what might have happened otherwise. We must be sure to tell them how grateful we are. And you'll want to thank them again yourself, I expect, Jack."

He nodded but said nothing. Mr. Steadman, who was reading the paper sitting on the veranda rail, glanced up at him curiously. He seemed about to speak, but thought better of it and turned back to his newspaper.

Later on he and Pat took Billy down for the morning swim. Mary and Tess were already there under their umbrella, and this time Mr. Steadman and Pat lay down under it with them while Billy got busy with his daily digging.

"How's Jack this morning?" asked Mary.

"Pretty right, I think," said Mr. Steadman. "His mother thought a morning at home wouldn't do him any harm, so we left him grumbling gently to himself in the hammock."

"He did take a bit of a beating yesterday," said Tess.

"We're more than grateful to you both for rescuing him so promptly," said Mr. Steadman. "Pat tells us you behaved in the most expert and exemplary manner."

"Well, we couldn't just sit there and let him drown, you know," said Tess in some surprise.

"It was rotten bad luck for the poor boy," said Mary.

"Bad judgment, more likely," said Mr. Steadman. "I understand you cautioned him about swimming too soon after a meal. And I've told him the same before. Perhaps he'll remember now."

"Oh well, we live and learn," said Tess sagely. "And it must be as strange for him here as it would be for us in the country."

"Have you never been to the country?" asked Mr. Steadman.

"No," said Tess. "Only a few holiday places, and they're not real country, are they?"

Mr. Steadman smiled. "No. I sometimes wonder if those holiday towns are real anything. Do you think you'd like the country if you're used to a city life?"

Tess wrinkled her forehead. "I couldn't say for sure, but

I think I should. Mary says it's awfully quiet, but I don't think I should mind that."

"You know the country, then?" said Mr. Steadman to Mary.

There was a trace of embarrassment on her serene face as she answered. "Not very well, really. But I have some friends on the Riverina I stayed with once. I—I—well, I was quite glad to get home again," she ended as tactfully as she could.

"Mary likes dances and things, you see," explained Tess. "I'm not supposed to be really old enough for them yet."

"Bad luck," said Mr. Steadman.

Tess grinned. "I don't mind. There are lots of other things you can do in town that are just as much fun. But I'll be a bit sick next week when we have to go back with still another ten days of holidays left. Mary has a string of dances lined up, but I'll miss this." She indicated the long, cool line of breakers.

"So will we," Pat suddenly said in heartfelt tones.

"Seems a pity you won't be able to console each other, doesn't it?" said Mr. Steadman, his eyes twinkling. "It must be an appalling fate to be faced with ten whole days with nothing to fill them. I can't remember when it last happened to me."

Pat looked up suddenly from the elaborate pattern she had been drawing on the sand, her round, freckled face alight with a newly born idea. "Father!" she said loudly in his ear.

"Hello?" he replied, startled. "What's happened?"

"I've had a wonderful idea."

"Oh," he said, and relaxed again. "What is it?"

"Couldn't Tess come back with us for the last ten days?"

"Come back with us? You mean to Pillana?" he asked in some surprise.

"Yes. If she'd like to, I mean. We could send her back on the plane. Couldn't we, Father?"

Mr. Steadman looked at her a little oddly for a moment, almost as if he were thinking of something else. Then he seemed to recollect himself, for he said, "It could be managed perfectly well. What about it, Tess? Would you like to try ten days in the bush?"

"I'd simply love it," Tess replied at once. "You're quite sure I wouldn't be in the way?"

"Not in the least," said Mr. Steadman. "If you'd really like to come, we'd be very pleased to have you. I've no doubt we could arrange to leave one of the tractors running outside your window at night if you felt it was a bit too quiet."

Tess gave him her quick smile and said, "Thank you very much, Mr. Steadman. If you promised to do that, I believe I might risk it." She turned to Mary. "I suppose it would be all right, Mary, wouldn't it? I don't think Mother would mind, do you?"

"I don't see why she should," said Mary. "In any case, you know what Mother is. She'll be so busy with her meetings and children's days and working bees, she'll never know whether you've gone or not."

"Oh, good," said Tess. "Neither she will. Mother," she explained to the others, "is bogged down in a children's library movement and really never notices you unless you have two covers, a binding, and a dust jacket."

"Or," added Mary, "unless you happen to be about two and a half, in filthy clothes and with rickets."

Mr. Steadman showed only polite interest at these revelations, but Pat looked bemused.

Tess laughed. "It's just that she's so awfully busy. She's always trying to think of about ten things at once, and if you ask her to pass the marmalade, she'll probably tell you she would if it had been Thursday, but she'll really have to put that aside until the Smithville general meeting is over."

"I daresay it sounds quite crazy to you," said Mary. "But you'd be surprised what a lot of good work she does. I think you'd like Mother," she added unexpectedly.

Mr. Steadman smiled. "I believe I should," he said.

"You'll come, then?" said Pat, beaming.

"Yes, thank you," said Tess. "I daresay I'd better just mention it to Mother. It will be an Experience."

It was arranged that as the Steadmans had to spend a couple of days in Sydney on their way home, they should pick Tess up there because, as she pointed out, a change of clothes would be necessary. Swimming outfits and sun-suits would hardly be suitable for the northwestern plains.

"Don't bring anything good, though," said Pat, thinking suddenly of the shabby old riding pants that were her own usual attire at home.

On their way home from the beach that morning, Pat tucked her hand in her father's arm and did a skip or two beside him.

"Isn't that a splendid idea, Father?" she said. "I'm so pleased Tess is coming."

Mr. Steadman nodded, but did not seem quite to be sharing his daughter's enthusiasm.

"Aren't you pleased, too?" she asked anxiously.

"Well," he said thoughtfully, his eyes on the road in front, "for myself I'm very pleased to have Tess if she wants to come. In a way it's the least we can do. But has it occurred to you at all that Jack might not be very pleased?" He looked around at her seriously.

"Jack?" said Pat in surprise. "After what happened yesterday, I didn't think he'd mind a bit. You don't think he will, do you, Father?"

"I believe he might," said Mr. Steadman.

"But surely he's grateful to Tess now?" said Pat.

"Naturally he is," said Mr. Steadman. "But you must remember that to be rescued from what I might call one's own folly by two very young ladies whom you've been in the habit of despising is a humiliating experience. Now if he'd rescued Tess, it would be very different."

"I never thought of that," said Pat in a small voice.

"I had," said Mr. Steadman. "That's why, when you first suggested it, I rather wondered for a moment. However," he said, stepping out more briskly, "we can trust him to behave, and even if he doesn't care much for the idea, it won't do him any harm to have to put up with it."

But Pat was thoughtful for the rest of the way home, and she had so much lost confidence in the idea that it was not she, but Billy, who eventually broke the news when they reached the cottage. In the middle of dinner he suddenly put down his spoon and fork and announced, "I'm sitting in the back with Tess and Pinkie when we go home."

"What did you say?" asked Jack with a frown.

"I'm sitting with Tess," repeated Billy patiently, "in the back. She said I could. And I shan't be sick, either," he added defiantly.

"What is all this?" asked Jack.

Pat caught her father's eye in silent appeal.

"It appears that Tess is rather at a loose end for the

rest of the holidays," said Mr. Steadman with deliberation. "We thought it would be a nice idea if she came
home with us and spent her last ten days at Pillana. So
we have asked her, and she is coming with us when we
go."

"What a very good plan," said Mrs. Steadman.

But Jack looked at his father in amazement. "You've
actually asked her home?" he said. "What on earth were
you thinking of? She's never been to the country in her
life."

"That's why," said Mr. Steadman.

"Well, you'd better put her off," said Jack abruptly.
"She'll be like a fish out of water."

"Oh, no," said Pat. "She said she'd love it. And you
don't really mind, do you, Jack?"

"I don't seem to have been given much choice, do I?"
he said, and went on with his dinner.

No more was said about it then, but Pat could feel, unhappily, the weight of Jack's disapproval.

The last two days came and went, and the weather
held for them until the end. The Moorlands went back to
Sydney the day before them, and they had their last swim
without the presence of the beach umbrella. They did not
realize until it had gone what a sense of assurance it had
given them in the weeks before.

The final day was a hectic one of sorting, packing, and
cleaning. Pinkie was put into and taken out of the utility
five times before he was eventually stowed by his solicitous owner, swathed in an old pajama jacket, in the glove
compartment.

"Pinkie likes a little room of his own," explained Billy
as he cast the contents of the glove compartment in a
heap on the floor.

Finally they drank their last cup of tea, put out the trash can, locked the front door, and climbed into the utility.

The long curve of the beach lay basking in the morning sun as they drove along the road for the last time. The big rollers still followed one another in from the sea to crash in showers of suds on the wet sand. The deep note of moving water that had been in their ears continuously for the past three weeks still went on. But they turned a corner, made their way inland, and ceased to hear it.

CHAPTER FOUR

Home to the Northwest

*T*hey picked up Tess in Sydney and began the four-hundred-fifty-mile journey home. Jack had prophesied that she would turn up with a mountain of assorted suitcases, and they were pleasantly surprised when she produced only one, and that of a reasonable size. It was packed in the back of the utility with the rest of the luggage. She and Pat got in the front with Mr. Steadman, while the rest of the family, with Mrs. Steadman driving, went in the car, which had been garaged in Sydney while they were at the seaside.

"Jack always goes with Mother," said Mr. Steadman, "so that he can give her a break at the wheel when we get out into the country."

The first stretch of their journey took them along the coast, through hilly, scrubby country with occasional rich valleys where tall timber grew and neat citrus orchards were laid out, familiar to them all from their recent holiday. They frequently passed through small towns, and everywhere there were signs of people holidaying or

busy about their daily work. But after a time they left
the coast and headed inland; the coastal scrub gave place
to clearer country with more open paddocks scattered
with cattle, and the tidy orchards were left behind for
good. After a time they lost the feeling that somewhere
near at hand beyond the hilltops lay the ocean.

By the time they stopped for the night, the air already
had the dry, crisp tang of the true country and, on this
still summer night, brought the scent of growing things
and hay.

The next day they crossed the Great Dividing Range.
The rivers no longer headed for the coast they had left,
but flowed now on their long journey toward the Darling, deep inland, to join the Murray and to meet the
ocean at last in South Australia. Bit by bit the country
opened out, the towns became fewer, and their way led
them along tree-lined watercourses through wide, undu-
lating plains. After a time even the creeks became fewer,
and midday found them driving steadily across dead flat
plain country shimmering with heat haze. Away in the
distance they could see the gray-blue mass of a mountain range.

"Do you see those hills?" Pat said to Tess.

"Yes," answered Tess. "I've been wondering what they
are."

"We're going to climb them in the September holidays,"
said Pat. "It was Jack's idea, and it's going to be such fun.
They're quite high and very rough and steep. We're to go
with packhorses and camp at the top, aren't we, Father?"

"So I've heard you say," replied Mr. Steadman. "I had
not planned to be one of the party. At my age I do not
willingly give up a bed, four walls, and a roof for the sake
of an energetic frolic on a mountaintop."

"I was hoping you'd come," said Pat. "I didn't think you'd mind sleeping on the ground when you're so used to it."

"That's the reason," said Mr. Steadman. "When you've done as much of it from necessity as I have, you don't take it on for pleasure. But I'm not trying to put you off."

"I think it sounds terribly exciting," said Tess. "An adventure!"

"Yes," said Mr. Steadman. "It should be what you would call, I think, an Experience. Those are the Karkoo Ranges, and I believe they are pretty well circular. Rather an odd formation, really, rising to such a height straight out of these vast, flat plains. The highest peak is Mount Calca, somewhere near the middle, and although they talk of opening them up someday, I understand there's nothing much there now but a few scrub cattle."

"Is there a road to the top?" asked Tess. "Or shall you have to blaze a trail?"

"Something between the two," said Mr. Steadman, smiling. "There's no road, but there are people living round about who will take you up. You'll have to ask Jack all about it. He's been making inquiries. He's had this idea at the back of his mind for some time."

"I think it's splendid," said Tess with enthusiasm. "They look so dreamy and mysterious, all mixed up with the sky and the haze like that." She continued to gaze with rapt interest at the distant range of hills until they slid behind and were lost to sight.

After that, as they drove steadily into the west, the afternoon grew hotter and hotter. The sun beat down through the windshield onto their laps, and except for an occasional grove of cypress pines all huddled together, it seemed for company, or a distant line of river gums along some hidden creek, there was not a tree or a shrub for shade. The road led on, flat, straight, and uneventful through a plain that appeared to have no end, and even the fences on either side had receded to allow a wider stock route. There appeared to be no limit in this vast expanse to either time or space, and Tess began to think they might drive on to infinity across the billiard-table flatness. They grew silent. The steady rhythm of the motor, as it spun them along mile after endless mile at the same even speed, lulled them to a trancelike stillness only broken when, at long intervals, they came to a small town huddling thirstily on the bank of a creek. Then there would be a flash of corrugated-iron and weatherboard houses past the windows, the blessed green of a tree or so, and out again onto the open plain with the town behind them as if it had never been.

Earlier in the day they had been able to see homesteads at fairly frequent intervals in the distant paddocks, but now the homestead units—a group of buildings, peppertrees, and windmill—appeared only very occasionally. Paddock fences ran across the country with geometric precision, bisecting each other neatly at right angles and carrying on without a bend or kink into the distance. At this time of year the tall grasses of the plains had been bleached to a pale parchment color and stood, crackling and aromatic, in the silence of the blazing afternoon.

Once Tess called out with pleasure, "Oh, look! A lake! How lovely. There are some cattle standing in the water."

But Mr. Steadman shook his head. "It's only the heat," he said. "It will disappear when we reach it. You wait." And presently, when they reached it, there was nothing but the same dusty road, the parchment grass, and the endless horizon.

"It's a mirage," said Pat. "Like they have in the Sahara."

At last when the heat of the day was over, the country began to change; the dead flatness of the plain gave place to slight undulations, here and there were outcrops of rock, and the homesteads became more frequent again. In the distance they could see ranges of low hills and among them clumps of trees. Little by little the land seemed to take heart, to thrive and to flourish. And now, with the fuchsia colors of evening streaming up the hollows, they came to wide, rolling pastureland cut by watercourses and patterned with the stubble of harvested crops.

"Nearly home now," said Pat.

"Oh, good," said Tess in such heartfelt tones that Mr. Steadman laughed and turned his head to look at her. "I suppose you thought we'd never stop," he said.

"I did," said Tess. "For a time I thought I'd spend the rest of my days going along that flat, straight road."

"It always seems like that," he said. "You're always a bit surprised when you come to the end."

The road ran now beside a railway line and, after about a mile, turned into the main street of a prosperous and busy little town. A few lights were on already, and groups of people stood about at street corners or at the open doorways of one or two cafés.

"Talia, our hometown," said Pat. "Only about twenty miles more."

Tess's eyebrows shot upward. "Your *home*town, did you say? Twenty miles away? Rather a long way to walk for the morning paper, isn't it?"

"It would be if we did," said Mr. Steadman. "But the papers come out with the mail twice a week."

"Ye gods!" said Tess, and relapsed into a stunned silence.

They left the town behind; the sounds of traffic, shouting children, and barking dogs became fainter as they slid into the dusk and the silence.

Presently they turned off the road, rattled over a ramp, and drove along a well-marked wheel track in a paddock thick with dry grass. In the light of the headlamps clumps of trees loomed up and vanished, and the dark shapes of cattle were outlined for a moment as they passed.

"This is our neighbor's property," said Mr. Steadman. "And a nice one, too."

"Only ours is nicer," said Pat quickly.

"Ours is home. That's the only difference," said Mr. Steadman.

They rattled over another ramp, and Pat bounced up in her seat. "This is Pillana," she said to Tess. "You'll see the house in a minute."

They swung off the track, took a smaller one that led through a thick clump of ironbarks, and came out suddenly onto a wide plain. On the far side some lights were twinkling.

"There!" said Pat.

Tess peered ahead with interest, but could make out only a low, dark mass pricked with lights. Against the faint glow of the horizon were the pointed tops of one or two tall trees.

Pat wriggled around, gathering up hats, coats, and an assortment of parcels that were piled on the ledge below the back window.

"No sign of the others behind us," she said, shading the window with her hand.

"Some way behind, I expect," said Mr. Steadman. "They wouldn't want to drive in our dust all day, and Mother will make Jack keep the pace down, if I know her."

The utility rolled smoothly across the plain, starting a hare that made off with great bounds and then veered out of the headlights and disappeared into the dark. A white fence showed up suddenly, and they swung around, crossed a ramp by a white gate, slid into the shadow of some trees, and stopped.

"All out," said Mr. Steadman, opening his door.

Tess opened hers and stepped out. The night was warm, but the air, light, dry, and scented, tingled in her nostrils. In the darkness she could not see much—the edge of a garden, the wall of a shed—but overhead the sky, remote and full of stars, stretched to infinity. Like the plains of the afternoon, it had no end and no beginning, but held her and all the quiet country around them in a wide and deep tranquillity. She drew a deep breath.

"I feel wonderful," she said.

Pat unwound herself from among the gear and brake levers, grasped an armful of varied articles, and climbed out after her.

"Come along," she said as she slid to the ground. "I'll show you your room. We wired Mrs. Battle, and she will have made up a bed for you."

"You'd better hurry up," said Mr. Steadman as he held the garden gate open for them. "I expect Mrs. Battle has a meal waiting for us, and you can take over from her when you're ready. She'll be wanting to get home."

As they crunched their way up the garden path, Tess,

with two suitcases, a kit bag under her arm, and two hats balanced on her head, said to Pat, "Don't tell me the unfortunate Mrs. Battle has to get herself back to Talia tonight."

"Oh, heavens, no," said Pat. "She lives only across the yard there. She's our head stockman's wife and just keeps an eye on things when we're away—and feeds Uncle John," she added as an afterthought.

They followed the path around a group of thick shrubs, the house loomed up in front of them, and they stepped onto a wooden veranda. With a sigh of relief Pat dumped her armful of belongings.

"We'll leave those there for the time being," she said, "and I'll show you your room."

Tess dropped one suitcase, the kit bag, and one of her hats and followed Pat along the veranda. It was illuminated dimly by the light from one or two curtained windows, and there seemed to be a great deal of it. Toward the far end they passed a small room on the outer edge of the veranda. Sounds of violently agitated water came through its closed door, and as they drew level, the quiet of the evening was shattered by a rich and powerful baritone voice suddenly uplifted in song.

"Ah Mimi, false, fickle-hearted!" the voice announced with deep feeling. Tess jumped.

"Whoever's that?" she muttered to Pat.

"Uncle John, having his bath," said Pat unconcernedly. "He always does that." They turned a corner and entered a dark hallway. Tess heard, dying away in the distance, Uncle John's voice in delicious anguish announcing, "Tra la la la . . . your beauty haunts me still."

Pat opened a door and switched on the light. "Here's

your room," she told Tess. "I'm next door, but I sleep on
the veranda. Our bathroom's just along here. It's a good
thing we don't share Uncle John's, isn't it?"

Tess laughed. "Your Uncle John doesn't suffer from
repressions, anyway."

Pat thought for a moment. "I don't believe he does,"
she said finally. She twitched the cover off Tess's bed
and went to the door. "I'll be along in the kitchen when
you're ready. Give a whistle when you come along the
veranda, and I'll show you where." She gave Tess her
wide, friendly smile and hurried off, and Tess heard her
purposeful footsteps becoming fainter up the long veranda.

The kitchen, when Tess eventually found it, was in a
separate building from the rest of the house, but opening
onto the same veranda so that it was not necessary to go
out into the open to reach the dining room. Mrs. Battle
had left, and Pat, looking small but competent beside
the large stove, was boiling eggs for Billy. By the time
they were ready and Tess, acting under instructions, had
made a large brown pot of tea, the others had arrived.

In a short time they were all assembled around the
long table in the dining room. Billy looked travel-worn
but cheerful, and announced as he climbed into his chair
that he wasn't a bit tired and did not propose to go to
bed for ages.

"We'll see," said Mrs. Steadman. "Get on with your
egg now, anyway."

They were all seated and were starting their meal
when the dining room door opened and a voice that
Tess recognized as the baritone from the bathroom said,
"Well, the travelers returned. And how was the ocean?
Wet as ever?"

Tess looked up to see a tall, broad-shouldered man, a little bald, but with alert, shrewd eyes and a humorous mouth. Although he resembled Mr. Steadman faintly, he did not look the true country-man his brother did. He had the air of someone more debonair and more worldly. He moved lightly and with a hint of swagger.

"Hello, Uncle John," chorused his nephews and niece.

"Good evening, John," said Mrs. Steadman. "I'm sorry if we've kept you waiting. We're a little later than I'd hoped."

"My dear Kathleen," he said, sitting down and shaking out his napkin, "I'm delighted to see you all back." His eye roved around the table. "You're all looking like redskins and remarkably fit, and—hello, who's this?" His glance rested on Tess, who returned it composedly, but her eyes sparkled.

"This is Tess Moorland, John," said Mrs. Steadman. "She's come up with us to sample the country life till school starts again. She and her sister were our neighbors at the seaside."

"Well, well," said Uncle John, with lively interest. "I should think, after this afternoon's drive, you're about ready to return to the city again, are you?"

"I did think, for a time, that I might be," admitted Tess. "It was very hot."

Uncle John nodded. "Hotter than the hobs of hell at this time of year. I doubt myself whether the holiday's worth the drive back."

"Oh, *yes*, Uncle John," said Pat. "It was lovely."

"We swam in the sp—sp—Specific Ocean," announced Billy.

"Good boy!" said Uncle John admiringly. "An excellent

effort. Try it without the 's' next time, and I'll have to admit your holiday has not been in vain."

"Things all right here?" asked Mr. Steadman, pushing his plate aside and holding out a hand for the cup of tea that was traveling unsteadily down the table.

"Right as a fiddle," replied his brother. "Good season, no fires so far, not too many flies in the sheep, and—oh, Christmas, no! I forgot." He dropped his knife and fork and leaned across to Mr. Steadman, an expression of deep concern on his face. "There is something rather serious."

Mr. Steadman and Jack both looked up.

"It's Felicity. She's not too good at all. Seemed to come on suddenly this morning. Wouldn't eat, seemed to be in great pain. I did everything I could, but by lunchtime I was so worried I got Simpson out to have a look at her."

"Oh? What did he say?" asked Mr. Steadman abruptly.

"He's not quite sure. Gave her an injection, tested her blood, did all the things, but said it could be any of several rather nasty complaints. He's coming out again in the morning. I don't mind telling you, I'm pretty worried. It couldn't have happened at a worse time."

"Rotten bad luck," said Jack. "I suppose her certificate hasn't gone down yet?"

"Too early for that," said Uncle John. "There were times today when I thought she might not last the night. She's up there with a rug on—imagine, in this heat! Johnson's keeping an eye on her, but I'll have to go up and see for myself before I go to bed."

Everyone at the table, even Billy, was listening in hushed and horrified silence. Tess looked from one to the other, her eyes like saucers. At last, in the solemn silence that followed Uncle John's last words, she asked in a low and sympathetic tone, "Who—who is Felicity? A relative?"

Jack burst into delighted laughter; it was the first time Tess had seen him laugh with real enjoyment. She looked at him with astonishment. All the others, she noticed, were smiling as well. Uncle John turned to her, and even he, so distressed a moment before, had a smile he was unable to conceal.

"She might well be, you know," he said. "And as a matter of fact, I have relatives whose ailments would cause me less anxiety. But Felicity is—ah—a cow."

"A cow!" said Tess as if it were a word she had never heard before.

"She's Pillana Felicity the Second," said Pat, with more than a touch of pride. "And she *mustn't* be ill just now."

"You see," said Uncle John, his face still alight with amusement, "she's our very special stud heifer, and she's going down to the Sydney Show in a few weeks, to bring glory and renown to the Pillana stud."

"Oh," said Tess, her tense face relaxing, "I thought for a moment it was something really serious."

"My dear child," said Uncle John. "It is something really serious—nothing more so. Imagine if she were to die—now!" Their smiles faded, and for a minute they all imagined.

Then Tess nodded. "Of course," she said. "I see now. It's just that it's all so—so different."

"An Experience," murmured Mr. Steadman from the foot of the table.

After that the meal was resumed with more composure. When they had nearly finished, Pat said to Jack, "We saw Mount Calca quite clearly today, Jack. Did you?"

"I thought I could pick her out," he replied. "But it's hard to be sure at that distance."

"Pat tells me you're going to climb up there one day soon," said Tess. "It sounds awfully exciting."

"Not till the spring," said Jack. "And I don't know about exciting. It'll be pretty rough, I expect."

"I should think it would be wonderful," said Tess with enthusiasm.

"I don't think you'd like it," said Jack decidedly.

Shortly afterward they left the table, and Mrs. Steadman hurried Billy off to bed while Pat, Tess, and Jack collected the dishes and washed up. Billy's wakefulness had begun to evaporate as his tummy became comfortably fuller, and now he followed Mrs. Steadman along the veranda without a word of protest. The others followed very soon, for it had been a long day.

Pat, returning from the bathroom in pajamas and slippers, popped her head around Tess's door to say good night. But Tess, her dark head placid on the pillow and mouth slightly open, was already asleep. It would not be necessary to bring the tractor around to her window tonight.

CHAPTER FIVE

Pillana

*T*he next morning when Tess woke, she looked around the unfamiliar room in some bewilderment before she remembered where she was. Everything was quiet, but it was already bright daylight, and beyond the veranda outside her window, she could see the sun blazing down on the green of the garden. Over the white rail of the garden fence, the wide plain that they had crossed the night before lay fresh and shining under the new day. She bounced up in bed and scratched her head, wondering. It did not look like thunder outside, yet she had a feeling it had been a distant rumble of thunder that had awakened her.

She was still puzzling when Pat's head appeared around the door.

"Awake already?" said Pat. "It's only six o'clock."

"Good morning," said Tess, moving over and patting the side of the bed invitingly. "I was wondering if I heard thunder."

Pat came in and sat down. "There's no thunder this morning. You must have dreamed it."

"I must have," said Tess. "But it woke me up."

"Oh," said Pat suddenly. "I know. It must have been the horses."

"Horses?" said Tess, and looked about in astonishment, almost as if she expected one to spring out from under the bed. "What would they be doing in here?"

"Not in here," Pat explained kindly. "Out in the paddock. They were being run up. They're put into the yards every morning so that the men can catch them."

"Oh," said Tess, and laughed. "Life is full of surprises in this part of the world, isn't it?"

"You'll get used to it," said Pat. "It's all very simple, really."

"I daresay," said Tess doubtfully. "But I can see I've got a lot to learn."

Later on, at breakfast, Uncle John said, "What are you two girls doing this morning?"

"Nothing special so far," said Pat.

"Geraldine and I are doing a bit of a run around, and I'll probably end up at the stud farm. Like to come?"

Pat looked inquiringly at her mother. "I can manage if you want to go," said Mrs. Steadman.

"Well, yes, thank you, Uncle John," she answered.

"Good. In about half an hour then, when I've had a look at Felicity. Johnson seems to think she's on the mend this morning, by the way."

"I'm so glad," said Mrs. Steadman. "She probably just ate something. Billy's always doing it."

"Well, I wish to goodness she'd stick to the menu," said Uncle John.

"Is—er—would Geraldine be another cow?" asked Tess warily.

"Oddly enough, no," replied Uncle John. "But more intelligent and willful than any cow."

Afterward as Pat and Tess passed the office on their way to the garage, Mr. Steadman called out to Tess, "You will find that driving with Uncle John in Geraldine is yet another Experience—very much so. I advise you to sit well back in your seat and relax."

"It's not as bad as that, really," said Pat as they went on. "None of Uncle John's accidents have ever been bad ones."

"Isn't that nice?" said Tess with growing alarm.

In the light of day Tess could see that the house was a long rectangle of weatherboard surrounded by the low-roofed verandas with which she was already familiar. There were various smaller buildings behind it; the kitchen and cook's quarters, dating from the days when Pillana had a cook as a matter of course, and house-maids as well; the bathrooms, the office, and the laundry, all placed in a haphazard manner, as if they had been built as afterthoughts when the the need for them arose. In front of the house lay the largest part of the garden with lawns of couch grass still green even in the height of summer, shady trees and shrubs, beds of rosebushes, and borders of small flowers. It was rambling and a little overgrown, but it was an oasis in the parched, hot plain that surrounded it. The long front of the house was divided from the garden by a gravel path trellised and shaded for its whole length by a grapevine whose main stems were as thick as a man's arm.

Pat and Tess crossed the garden and went out of the small gate by which they had entered the previous night. On the other side of the yard was the garage, a long shed with double doors for the cars at one end only.

The rest was open and housed a remarkable collection of vehicles and farm machinery, all, to Tess's urban eye, in urgent need of a good wash. One pair of double doors stood open, and from the darkness inside came an earth-shattering roar, while clouds of smoke belched out into the still morning air.

"That's Geraldine," said Pat unnecessarily. As she spoke, Geraldine shot out backward and came to rest, vibrating eagerly under a pepper tree on the opposite side of the yard. She was an open tourer of ancient and honorable vintage. Uncle John's head peered around the windshield.

"Come on, you two," he shouted. "Jump in."

They jumped in beside him, and before Pat had closed the door, Geraldine leaped forward and headed for the ramp that lay between them and the open plain. She missed the side rail by inches, bounded over a dry gutter on the far side, and gathered speed as she turned onto a well-worn track across the plain.

Uncle John leaned back, one hand lightly on the wheel and a smile of contentment on his face.

"She knows the road," he said affably to Tess. "I don't have to do much, really."

"Oh, yes?" said Tess politely. "Where are we going? Or does Geraldine know that, too?"

Uncle John, much struck by this point, pondered for a moment, a faint frown creasing his forehead. Then he turned to Tess. "She may, you know," he said. "Quite likely, considering how often I drive over to the wool-shed."

Geraldine swerved off the track and plunged purpose-fully into the long grass at the side. A solitary ironbark stood in her path.

"Tree!" said Pat as if she had said it many times before.

Uncle John looked ahead, swung the wheel, and Geraldine bounded onto the track once more. They reached the end of the open plain without misadventure, crossed another ramp, and headed for a line of trees.

"This is the woolshed creek," said Uncle John as Geraldine tipped forward and rattled down a short, sharp bank into the bed of the creek.

"But it's dry!" said Tess as they crossed the sandy bottom.

"Well, of course," said Uncle John in surprise. "We couldn't cross it if it weren't, could we?"

"They're always dry except in the rain," said Pat. "We get our water from bores."

The track led diagonally up the steep bank on the other side. But Geraldine, apparently sensing that Uncle John's attention was on a group of cattle standing in the shade farther down the creek, took the opportunity to charge headlong at the bank.

"Hey!" said Uncle John, changing gear quickly and stamping on the accelerator. They roared up, labored slightly near the top, and crawled onto the level.

"Climbs like a cat, doesn't she?" he said proudly.

A little way ahead, on higher ground, stood a large corrugated-iron building. From the yards surrounding it rose a cloud of dust. Above the roar of Geraldine, Tess could hear dogs barking.

"That's the woolshed," said Pat.

They passed a plantation of dark, cool-looking cypress pines on their right, swung around a corner of the fence, and stopped beside the woolshed. Geraldine pulsated gently, a shimmer of heat rising off her radiator. Uncle

John leaned out and called to a big, thickset man stand-ing by the yards, "Those the ones I want, Tom?"

The man nodded and pointed to the yards, which seethed with a packed and moving mass of sheep. Uncle John switched off the engine and got out. "Come on, you two," he said. "I may need you."

Pat and Tess climbed out. The sun beat down on their heads, and a cloud of little flies settled on their faces.

"Don't yawn," said Pat, "or you'll swallow one."

They followed Uncle John over to the yards and stood leaning over the rail, watching the sheep while he talked to Tom. Two or three dogs lay panting in the shade by the rail, and the sheep, their sides heaving, stood re-signedly, each with its head low in an effort to make use of the shade of its neighbor. After a few minutes Uncle John and Tom climbed over the rail into the yard. The dogs, alert at once, jumped over after them. They pushed their way through the first big yard of sheep and opened the gate into a smaller yard that led into a long, narrow race. Uncle John walked up to the head of the race and waited.

"Come on, now," he called to Pat. "Lend a hand."

Tom already had the small yard full of sheep and, with the aid of his dogs, was urging them up the race.

"He's going to draft this lot," said Pat as she climbed into the yard. "All we've got to do is get them into the small yard for Tom."

"Oh," said Tess as she followed Pat into the yard. "I suppose they don't bite or anything."

"They might knock you over if you're not looking, that's all," said Pat, laughing. "The poor dears get so hot and bothered."

"They're not the only ones," said Tess, whose face under her felt hat was already turning deep pink.

For half an hour or so Pat and Tess urged, prodded, and shouted at the sheep, moving them up into the small yard as they were required. The dogs barked without ceasing and rushed about in a businesslike way that Tess envied, achieving more with one quick dart and a yelp of excitement than she could with twice the amount of energy and noise. Pat moved about methodically, Tom prodded them with encouraging noises up the race, and Uncle John stood in silent concentration at the far end, moving first one gate and then another, sorting the sheep into different mobs as they came up one by one. The dust rose up like a pall, and the little flies clung lovingly around mouth and eyes. And over it all the sun blazed down ceaselessly.

When the last sheep was through, Tess pushed back

her hat and leaned against the rail. Her face was bright red and damp, and when she brushed her forehead with the back of her hand, the clinging dust made brown streaks. Uncle John walked toward the girls with a jaunty step.

"Well, that's that," he said. "And how do you like sheep work, Tess?"

"Oh, great fun," said Tess weakly.

"Thought you'd enjoy a taste of it," he said. "But you've got to remember it's not all fun. Sometimes it's quite hard work. Isn't it, Pat?"

"Sometimes," said Pat. "But I always like it."

"So you do," said Uncle John. "I've always said you take after your father. But as a matter of fact," he went on confidentially to Tess, "cattle are my first love. Give me a nice herd of shorthorns any day. Come along; we'd better get going or we'll never be home in time for lunch."

They went on past the woolshed, traveling through one paddock after another until Tess felt hopelessly lost. She had no idea where the homestead lay or where they might be heading. Once, as they made their way through a fairly heavily timbered paddock, they came upon a little rocky hill that jutted suddenly from the level ground for no apparent reason and reared itself high above the surrounding trees. Small, stunted trees grew on its steep sides.

"That's Sugarloaf," said Pat. "There's a lovely view from the top. We'll climb it one day."

For a moment Tess's heart sank as she looked at its rugged slopes. There seemed to be no track anywhere. Then she drew a deep breath and nodded brightly. "Good," she said. "That will be nice."

"There are lots of hills like that in this district," said Uncle John. "And they're all called Sugarloaf. A sad lack of imagination, I always think."

They came to a paddock where groups of fat red cattle stood about in the shade of the trees. Here their progress became more erratic. Uncle John lost interest in the track and headed Geraldine for one group after another to gaze with absorbed interest at each.

"These are the stud cows," said Pat. "They're Uncle John's special pets."

"Something made me think they must be," said Tess.

Uncle John looked at her with interest. "Did it really?" he said. "Perhaps you have a natural eye for cattle. They're certainly nice-looking beasts."

"Oh, I don't think I have," Tess was forced to admit. "I only know which is the front by the horns."

"Never mind," said Uncle John. "Some people have a natural instinct. You see you noticed at once that these were out of the ordinary."

Tess decided it would be best to accept the "natural eye" bestowed on her by Uncle John and said no more.

Shortly afterward they skirted the edge of a patch of scrub and came in sight of a cottage with several orderly wooden sheds behind it. There were a number of small rectangular yards about the sheds, surrounded by high, solid post-and-rail fences.

"Where are we now?" asked Tess, who began to think that home and lunch were farther away than ever.

"This is the stud farm," said Pat. "Johnson, the stud groom, lives here with the bulls."

"Dear me!" said Tess involuntarily.

The glimmer of a smile appeared on Uncle John's

face. "Of course he has his wife with him as well," he explained.

"*And* three children," said Pat.

They crossed one or two paddocks and stopped beside the sheds. Uncle John stepped out.

"You two can have a look around if you like," he said. "I'm just going to have a word with Johnson and look at Felicity again." He strode off without waiting for a reply.

"You'd like to see the bulls, wouldn't you?" Pat asked.

"Yes, *please*," said Tess, feeling that any other answer would put her beyond the pale.

Pat led the way into the yards. In the nearest, two or three young bulls were tied in the shade at intervals along the fence. To Tess they seemed almost indecently fat, but she was pleased to notice that none of them appeared to be at all ferocious; they all, in fact, looked sleepy and contented and not at all disposed to do anything in a hurry. In one corner a fourth was having a bath and stood placidly enough while a boy of about Jack's age, in an open shirt, shorts, and boots, rubbed his rough, wet coat with a currycomb.

"These ones are all about six months old," said Pat. "They're being made ready for the Show." She walked about among them, patting a back here and rubbing a nose there in an unconcerned manner that filled Tess with admiration. Tess did her best to appear at ease as she followed Pat, but she jumped back quickly as one of the bulls swung around to look at her, and to her annoyance she noticed the boy glance across at her and grin. She pulled herself together and marched up to Pat, forcing herself to put out her hand and rub the bulging neck as Pat was doing. But her action was a bit too quick; the bull rolled his eye at her and moved away against the fence. Again, before she could stop herself, she stepped back, but Pat, who had not moved, smiled reassuringly.

"He's just not used to strangers yet," she explained. "They're quite quiet really."

After that they walked through the other yards, Pat describing the occupants as they went. To Tess, who privately thought one bull looked very much like another, it seemed almost miraculous the way Pat knew without hesitation each of some fifteen to twenty beasts, its past history, ancestry, and probable future. Here, on her own ground, Pat was a very different person from the one Tess had learned to know at the seaside.

In the last yard they came to, a huge bull, twice the size of the others they had seen, stood tied to a pepper-tree by a ring through his nose. He was rubbing the flies off his eyes on the bark. As they drew near, he emitted a deep, ominous rumble from somewhere in the depths of his interior. In spite of her determination, Tess hesitated, but a voice behind her said, "Poor old fellow, he wants his dinner." And Uncle John appeared.

Tess turned to him with a vague feeling of relief. "This one is a giant," she said. "He's a whole mountain on his own, really."

"Isn't he," agreed Uncle John, walking up to the bull and putting an arm lovingly around the great neck. The bull rumbled again. "He's our pride and joy, this one. Let me introduce you to Pillana Centaur—we hope shortly to be able to add Grand Champion. He's two years old now, but I'll tell you a secret; he's still a great baby at heart and takes his milk every day from a foster mother."

"Good heavens," said Tess, scandalized. "He must need a she-elephant to keep him going."

Pat laughed. "You'd think so, wouldn't you? But she's only a little Jersey cow. The silly old thing has to get down on his knees, and even then he nearly knocks her over."

"So you see," said Uncle John. "Although he looks pompous, it's only skin deep."

Tess, made bold by these revelations of Centaur's homelife, walked up to him and patted his back. It was like patting a bank. As they stood there, a small black cat walked along the top rail of the fence, arched its back, and rubbed along the bull's wet lifted nose. As it sauntered on, the bull opened his mouth and closed it on the cat's tail. The cat immediately turned, in annoyance rather than fear, and rapped the bull smartly on the nostril with one front paw. The bull let go, and the cat strolled on.

"You see?" said Uncle John as they laughed. "Even old Tom has him bluffed."

Soon afterward Uncle John looked at his watch and announced that they had ten minutes to get home before lunch.

"I always think," said Uncle John as they rattled home, "that driving fast in Geraldine is like riding in an airplane."

They raced up the yard, swerved around, and dived into the garage. Uncle John pulled out his watch again.

"Ten minutes flat," he said. "Not bad going." He patted Geraldine on the spare tire with much the same affectionate gesture that he had used on Pillana Centaur.

The family assembled again for lunch. Billy looked a

little pensive and toyed more fastidiously than usual with his chop.

"Billy has been helping me bottle," said Mrs. Steadman. "He's been so useful."

"Billy's always an asset at fruit bottling," said Mr. Steadman. "He serves much the same function as a crow in the paddock. Eats anything nobody else wants."

"And regrets it afterward," said Jack as his young brother pushed the plate away with distaste.

"And how did you enjoy yourself?" Mrs. Steadman asked Tess.

"We had a most exciting time," replied Tess. "Sheep, bulls—and Geraldine."

"I believe that Tess has a natural eye for cattle," said Uncle John. "She spotted the stud cows at once."

"Oh, no, really. I—" began Tess. But Jack interrupted her.

"Impossible. She doesn't know anything about cattle—do you?" he asked suspiciously. Tess shook her head.

"One doesn't have to know," said Uncle John. "It's an instinct. One is born with it, or one is not. You're not," he added unkindly. "Pat may be; I'm not sure yet. I am, happily."

"Nevertheless," said Mr. Steadman mildly, "you must have a little experience, and I hardly think—"

"I don't believe it," said Jack. "You talk as if it were like an ear for music—or a good style at cricket. How does she know what to look for?"

"It is," said Uncle John impressively. "It's exactly like an ear for music, only much more important, naturally. You mark my words; this girl will pick out a champion one day."

"I'd rather she picked out a few likely rams for my flock ewes," said Mr. Steadman.

"I really don't think I'd be much good at picking anything," said Tess when she could make herself heard. "I'm just beginning to find out how little I know about the country."

"Well," said Mr. Steadman, "don't be led away by those fat bulls up there. If it wasn't for my sheep, we couldn't afford to pay for their feed."

"Ah," said Uncle John soulfully. "No doubt a sheep can give you bread and butter, if that's all you want, but there's nothing like a good herd of cattle to refresh the spirit."

"You look after the spirit, then," said Mr. Steadman. "And I'll supply the bread and butter."

"And so between them both, you see, they licked the platter clean," said Mrs. Steadman from the head of the table. "This is a terrible household, Tess. We have this sheep and cattle business all the time. You'd better decide now which side you'll be on."

"Pinkie has a big bull tiger," said Billy, not to be outdone. "It gets champion at the Show every year."

"No competition, I suppose," said Mr. Steadman.

"Natural eye, indeed," muttered Jack, glaring at his uncle. But he was in a better humor with Tess after her frank confession, and he suddenly said, "Tell you what; I'll run Dreadnaught up for you tomorrow morning, Tess, and you can have a go on him."

"Oh?" said Tess, mystified but polite. "Thank you very much."

"Oh, I don't think Dreadnaught would be any good," said Pat. "He's too small, and much too fat."

"He may be," said Mr. Steadman. "But he'll be the best for Tess to start on."

"*I* don't mind if she uses Dreadnaught," said Billy handsomely. "He's mine, but she can have him."

"I like that," said Jack. "He was mine before he belonged to any of you."

"Who is Dreadnaught?" asked Tess, feeling she must know.

"How tantalizing it all is for you," said Mrs. Steadman. "They never explain anything, do they? Dreadnaught is the pony they all learned to ride on. He's old and fat, and he shies a bit, but you haven't far to fall, and he's very quiet, really."

CHAPTER SIX

A
Stranger
Outback

So the next morning after breakfast they made for
the yards, and Tess was introduced to Dreadnaught and
was reassured by what she saw. He was standing against
the fence, one leg resting and his head hanging. His
only sign of life was his tail, which switched from side
to side as the flies tried to settle on his flanks. He was
a taffy with a silver mane and tail, and his nose was
gray with age. He did not look in the least alarming.

There were two other horses in the yard as well, a
small, lightly built bay with a pretty, intelligent head,
and a big chestnut with a wild and suspicious eye. At
this time of year their coats were sleek and shining, and
they were a pleasant sight, Tess thought, as they stood
dreaming in the shade of the pepper trees.

Jack came up to the yards with them, for they were
to go out mustering with him, and Billy followed behind
because he disliked missing anything. Pinkie was borne
along under Billy's arm because he didn't like missing
anything either.

"The bay one's mine," said Pat as they approached the

yard. "His name's Turpin—after the highwayman, you know. The chestnut is Polly Perkins, and she's Jack's. She's a bit flighty, and nobody likes to ride her but Jack."

Pat carried Tess's bridle and her own, but when they got into the yard, Billy put Pinkie carefully on the corner post and announced that he would put the bridle on Dreadnaught himself. "Because he knows me," he explained. "And I can show Tess how." So Pat handed over the bridle, and Billy marched importantly up to Dreadnaught. The pony turned his head in mild interest as Billy approached and made soft welcoming noises through his distended nostrils. Tess was touched and reassured. But it appeared that his regard for Billy was mixed with caution, for when Billy went to put the bit in his mouth, he raised his head just sufficiently to be out of reach.

"Could I—?" said Tess, going forward uncertainly.

But Billy shook his head violently. "You old son of a gun," he muttered, and slung the reins around Dreadnaught's neck. Then he climbed up to the top rail of the fence, dragged the pony's head toward him, and slipped in the bit. When the bridle was firmly on and the throatstrap buckled, he climbed down and handed the reins to Tess.

"There you are," he said nonchalantly. "He knows me, you see."

Tess took them rather as if they were charged with an electric current.

By this time Jack and Pat had caught their horses, and Turpin was already saddled. Pat, explaining as she went, picked up Tess's saddle, threw it across Dreadnaught's fat little back, and pulled up the girth.

"With Dreadnaught," she said, "you won't really have to do anything but just sit there. He'll follow the other horses. You just want to watch in case he shies. He's a bit naughty that way, and he does it for fun."

"A misplaced sense of humor, I call it," said Tess, who was not sure that she would recognize a shy when she saw it, but felt sure it must be something unpleasant.

Jack was grooming Polly Perkins, who had been rolling in the dam and still wore patches of mud here and there.

"You might as well have a go while you're waiting," Pat said to Tess. So Tess walked up to Dreadnaught and, acting under instruction from Pat, grasped the reins, put her foot in the stirrup, hopped for a considerable time on her spare leg, and then plunged at the saddle. For a moment she clung like a limpet to the pommel, then, slowly but with gathering speed, the saddle rolled around toward her, depositing her seated on the ground somewhere between Dreadnaught's two front legs. Dreadnaught staggered for a moment to regain his balance and then stood patiently while Tess clambered to her feet and the saddle was readjusted. He had the resigned air of one who can no longer be surprised.

"You can't always expect the saddle to come to you," said Jack from under his horse's neck. "Next time, you try to go to it."

"It's because he's so fat," said Pat more kindly. "I'll try to girth him up tighter this time."

"Pinkie rides them bareback, without a bridle, even," shouted Billy from a vantage point beside the corner post.

For the first time Tess, glancing for a moment at the disreputable, bowlegged lamb standing serenely on the post, felt a mild resentment toward the indomitable Pinkie.

"Now," said Pat, handing her the reins again. "Put your hand on the other side of the saddle so that it won't roll and just spring up and swing your leg over."

"And roll a cigarette in one hand while I'm doing it, I suppose," said Tess bitterly, and she approached Dreadnaught for the second time. But she was determined not to be beaten twice, and this time she leaped on with such agility that Pat had to hold with all her might to her nearside leg to stop her going right over.

"I've read about people doing that," said Tess, panting a little as she regained her balance. "But I always thought it was like slipping on a banana skin; no one ever really *does*."

"Well, you didn't," said Pat. "Now ride him up to the night paddock fence and back till Jack's ready. If he won't go, kick him in the ribs. He'll hardly feel it, anyway."

So Tess, steering Dreadnaught rather as if the reins were tiller lines, made her uncertain way out of the yard gate and into the paddock. He did not like leaving the other horses and moved reluctantly, Tess's long legs giving spirited encouragement on either side. Jack finished saddling Polly Perkins and came to stand beside Pat, his elbows on the fence, the reins over his arm.

"It's delaying us a little," he said. "But as a morning's entertainment it's worth it."

"She's doing jolly well for the first time," said Pat indignantly.

"I will say," agreed Jack handsomely, "she's going to ride or bust. She'll be a sticker."

By now Dreadnaught had reached the fence. He

seemed to assume that he had come to his journey's end, for he stood with one leg resting, gazing out through the netting at the wide plain beyond. Tess pulled first one rein and then the other, but Dreadnaught only leaned his head a little to one side or the other. Tess screwed around in the saddle and called out, "What do I do now? He seems to have had enough."

"Pull him round and give him a good kick," shouted Jack. "He's only fooling you."

So Tess pulled and kicked with a will, and presently Dreadnaught heaved a sigh and moved off. This time his head was toward the other horses, and some of his extreme weariness left him. He walked along briskly.

"Give him a kick and make him trot," called Jack. So Tess dug in her heels again, and Dreadnaught obligingly broke into a gentle trot.

"Rise in your stirrups," shouted Pat as Tess bounced up and down like a tennis ball.

"I am," gasped Tess, cannoning off the saddle for the twentieth time. Considering how rapidly and violently she was rising, it seemed a pointless instruction. She had just begun to feel the rhythm of the movement when she passed Billy seated on the rail beside the corner post.

"Hurray!" screamed Billy, flinging his arms out with enthusiasm. One outstretched hand caught Pinkie a sharp tap in the ribs, and Pinkie, propelled into sudden life, sprang off the post and landed with a soft plop under Dreadnaught's nose.

Dreadnaught's head went up, his ears pricked, and he swerved to one side. But not Tess. She hung for a moment over space, clutching desperately at reins and mane, and then sat down heavily on Pinkie. A small cloud of dust rose up around her.

"Oh," shrieked Billy in dismay, sliding down from the rail. "Poor Pinkie!"

Pat ran over to Tess. "Are you hurt?" she asked.

"I am not," said Tess, getting slowly to her feet with a face like thunder. "But if that lamb were mutton, I'd— I'd *eat* it."

Over by the horses Jack was standing with his forehead resting on his forearms. When he lifted his head, Tess saw that his face was bright with happiness and tears of joy had wet his cheeks.

"All right, laugh," she said with furious dignity. "But I didn't laugh when you fell out of the boat."

"But your sister did, and I can't help it," said Jack, and burst into another paroxysm.

A reluctant smile crept into Tess's stormy face. "Oh, well," she said, "here I go again." She walked up to Dreadnaught, who stood patiently as he always did when riders left him unexpectedly, picked up the reins, and this time got on with less trouble than before.

"We'd better get a move on now," said Jack, and flung the reins over Polly's neck. Tess watched with envy as he swung onto the sidestepping, restless mare. Pat hopped onto Turpin, and they rode out onto the plain. Billy hung over the gate and gazed after them. Pinkie, for the moment overlooked even by his solicitous owner, lay in the dust where he had fallen.

This time Dreadnaught pattered along quite happily between the other two horses, and Tess had no trouble.

"We've only got to muster one paddock," said Jack as they rode along. "It won't take very long. You'd better keep Tess with you, Pat, and go round by the pines. I'll do the dam and the creek and meet you at the gate."

"All right," said Pat, and then, struck by a thought, she

turned and looked behind them. "Where's Silver?" she asked.

"Isn't he here?" asked Jack, looking around as well. "I let him go when I went over to the yards."

"Who is Silver?" asked Tess.

"Jack's border collie," said Pat. "He usually does all the work when we muster sheep, so we can't go without him."

"The best sheep dog in the Northwest," added Jack, "with a pedigree as long as next year." Satisfied that Silver was not with them, he put two fingers in his mouth, took a deep breath, and produced a whistle that nearly cracked Tess's eardrums. He waited for a moment, peering back down the track, and then whistled again. This time a small black object and a puff of dust could be seen not far from the yards they had left.

"He's coming," said Jack. "But—" He stopped, puzzled.

Pat twisted around to look, too. "What's wrong with him?" she asked. "Is he lame? He's running in such a funny way."

"Not lame," said Jack, still staring. "There's a grayish sort of blob in front of him. Can't make it out. His head seems to be right up in the air."

The dog was coming nearer now, and Pat said suddenly, "He's got a rabbit in his mouth. Where on earth could he have caught it so near the house?"

"You're right," said Jack. "It does look like a rabbit." Then, as Silver emerged clearly from the tall grasses that fringed the track, he relaxed and grinned. "We might have guessed," he said resignedly. "It's Pinkie."

"Pinkie!" Tess's voice was almost a squeak. "Am I to be haunted forever by that lamb?" With an effort she turned, too. There was no doubt now. Silver, eager, ingratiating, and struggling with his load, came up to the horses, and over Pinkie's moist and dusty body his eyes rolled upward to Jack, awaiting the word of praise. Jack pulled up and got off. Almost before he had time to reach for it, the lamb was thrust into his hand. He bent and patted his dog. "Good boy," he said, with what seemed to Tess quite unnecessary enthusiasm.

Silver, his duty discharged, leaped and gamboled around the horses, a squirming mass of shaggy black-and-white border collie with pricked ears and amber eyes. When Jack mounted and they started off again, Silver bounded on ahead to inspect points of interest along the route, virtue obvious in every jaunty movement of the feathered tail.

"Here," said Jack, and handed Pinkie to Pat.

"Oh, bother," she said mildly, and tucked him under her arm.

After a moment's silence Tess asked in a bemused voice, "Is Pinkie really necessary for mustering sheep?"

"Good heavens, no," said Jack. "A darned nuisance. But we daren't let him get lost. Billy would never forgive us."

"Then why did you pat Silver for bringing him?" persisted Tess, determined to find logic somewhere.

"Well, he brought him, didn't he?" said Jack reasonably. "It might have been my saddlebag, or my stockwhip, or something that we really did want. You can't expect a dog to know the difference. There's not many dogs would have brought him at all."

"You see," said Pat, "Silver has a habit of bringing along anything Jack leaves lying about. It's rather clever of him, we think. And it's sometimes very useful. The trouble is that he's found it such a successful trick, with

Jack patting him and telling him what a good dog he is, that now he sort of can't stop. He turns up with all sorts of funny things sometimes. And of course Jack has to pat him just the same because he means so well."

"I see," said Tess, and wondered that anyone as impatient as Jack could be so patient with his animals.

"I expect Billy must have forgotten Pinkie when he went back to the house," said Pat. "Silver would never have dreamed of taking him from Billy."

"That dog," said Jack, "is worth a right arm to me."

"He must be," said Tess warmly. "I just didn't understand. He's a darling."

Jack looked at her with some scorn. "He's a working dog, not a pet," he said.

Pat laughed. "Jack always pretends he only likes him because he works well," she said. "But I remember one night when he didn't come back after we'd been doing sheep, and Jack spent most of the night riding round to see if he'd gotten caught in a fence."

"Can't afford to lose a good dog," said Jack gruffly.

"Was he all right?" asked Tess.

"Of course he was," said Pat. "He'd only eaten some of the shearers' dinner and was too full to come home."

After that they parted company. Jack whistled Silver and rode off toward the line of trees that marked the creek, and Pat and Tess turned their horses in the opposite direction. For a long time they moved up and down a wide area of country, and when they came across a mob of sheep, Pat would begin to utter the most extraordinary series of noises Tess had ever heard. She was not at all surprised when the sheep, hearing them, gave one startled look and made off hurriedly in the other direction. As they worked, the sun became hotter, the horses' necks grew damp, and the little flies clung to them with suicidal affection. After a time Tess felt that her neck muscles had grown weary of supporting her head, the small of her back ached, and there seemed to be altogether too much friction where she met the saddle. Dreadnaught, stamping along on his short legs, had to take about three strides to Turpin's one and gave her, in consequence, an uneasy ride.

As the morning wore on, the sheep became less and less inclined to move and, when they came to a patch of shade, would huddle in it, panting, until the riders were almost upon them.

Pat's round face flamed, and her voice was cracking. Tess was already speechless and would have asked permission to get off and walk, but a sudden memory came to her of Pat, half drowned, but dogged and uncomplaining as she struggled with her swimming lessons; and she painfully straightened the kink in her back and said nothing.

At last they got their sheep together and came within sight of the gate. Away on the other side they could see a tumbling creamy wave rolling toward them over a long rise. A cloud of dust hovered over it, and moving swiftly up and down across its rear was a small black-and-white dog.

"That's where Silver comes in handy," said Pat, pointing. "He's doing all the work, you see."

To Tess, sitting wearily on a pony that appeared to suffer from chronic hiccups, hot, aching, and hoarse, it seemed miraculous that any dog should know so exactly what was expected of it. She began to understand a little why Jack put such a high value on his Silver. To her surprise, as Jack's mob drew near the gate and almost

level with their own, he left his position at the rear and
cantered up around them to open the gate. Silver, in
complete control, brought them on of his own accord.
At the gate the two mobs met, and as they began to
stream through, Jack rode over to the girls.

"I want you to ride on when they're through and clear
the track," he said to Pat. "I'll keep an eye on Tess."

So as soon as she could get her pony through the gate,
Pat left them and rode on ahead, cantering easily through
the long, dry grass in a way that Tess felt she would
never be able to do.

Jack, glancing across at her, noticed the drooping back,
the weary, hot face, and the uncomfortable, unrelaxed
way in which she sat, and asked, more kindly than he
usually did, "Tired, Tess?"

She smiled and tried to sit up straighter. "A bit, but
I'm all right, really."

"Dreadnaught's a cow of a ride. Later on you can
have something a bit more comfortable."

"I'm afraid it's me that's the trouble, not Dreadnaught,"
said Tess, and Jack was forced to admire her honesty.

Eventually the bleating, milling mass of sheep in front
of them reached their destination, and when the last
panting animal was pushed into the yards and the gate
shut, Jack whistled Silver and they turned their horses
for home. It was obvious now that poor Tess was very
tired. She replied cheerfully enough when spoken to and
was always ready with her quick smile, but there were
long periods when she rode along with her mouth set,
saying nothing.

About halfway home Silver put up a rabbit in a tussock just by the track. It bounded up in front of Dread-
nought, who was a little behind the others. He side-

stepped in surprise; it was scarcely a shy, and Pat would hardly have noticed it, but it was enough for Tess in her present condition, and for the third time that morning she parted company with Dreadnaught. This time she did it with more deliberation and came to rest gently in the tussock the rabbit had left. But it was too much, and when Pat got off and walked up to her, she burst into tears.

"Oh," said Pat in alarm. "Jack, quick! She's hurt herself."

Jack swung off Polly Perkins and came up in two strides. But to their surprise Tess scrambled to her feet and in broken tones, blinking furiously, addressed them.

"You silly idiots, I'm *not* hurt. How could I be hurt falling onto a tussock? Don't look at me in that stupid way. I suppose I can fall off if I want to? You may think

I'm crying, but I'm not. I wouldn't be such a fool." She stopped, pulled herself together, and with her head in the air stalked majestically past them. Dreadnaught still waited where his few unpremeditated steps had taken him, and she took hold of the reins, put her foot into the stirrup, and with a mighty spring got herself into the saddle. They saw her set her teeth as she took the weight off the stirrups. In silence Pat and Jack returned to their horses, flung the reins over, and got on. In silence they proceeded homeward.

They were in sight of the homestead gate when there came a brisk thudding behind them, and Dreadnaught, who had dropped back when they started off, drew level with their horses.

"I'm sorry I behaved like that," said a remarkably meek voice, and they both looked around, a little sheepishly, to see Tess riding beside them, the ghost of a smile on her face.

Pat beamed with pleasure, and Jack, with a grin he was quite unable to conceal, said with surprising tact, "Don't apologize and don't explain. I know just how you felt."

When they reached home, they found Billy wandering disconsolately around the yards, a figure of forlorn dejection. He looked up as they rode in, and they noticed that his eyes were red and his face had a sodden appearance.

"I can't find Pinkie," he said without preliminary. Then his eye fell on Pat and the dusty object under her arm. Despair fell away, and he darted forward, causing Turpin to snort and sidestep.

"Steady now," said Pat as she handed Pinkie down.

"Why did you take him?" said Billy angrily. "I never said you could."

"She didn't, you ass," said Jack. "You left him behind, and Silver brought him. You know he always does."

"Oh," said Billy, falling on the panting Silver in an excess of misplaced gratitude, "you clever, clever dog." And, all grievance forgotten, he clutched Pinkie to his chest and ran toward the house.

Fortunately for Tess's peace of mind they were late for lunch, and the others had left the table. It appeared that Billy, questioned closely by Uncle John, had given a vivid account of proceedings up to the time when they left the yards, but points of view vary, and Mr. and Mrs. Steadman had been left with the impression that the worst of the calamities during that period had befallen Pinkie, and that the worst calamity of all was that he was now missing. Tess was relieved to find that both Pat and Jack were tactfully noncommittal about the morning's exploits, and the full story was told only to Mrs. Steadman, who had immediately noticed Tess's jaded appearance. She was horrified and full of sympathy.

"You poor girl," she said. "You must be black and blue, as well as exhausted. You must go and have a rest immediately and a good hot bath before you go to bed tonight, and don't get up to breakfast tomorrow if you don't feel like it. I never heard of such a silly thing— taking you all that way for your first ride, and after you'd fallen off twice, too!"

She started to scold Pat and Jack so wholeheartedly that Tess was obliged to come to their rescue.

"Oh, but I enjoyed it, Mrs. Steadman. I wouldn't have missed it for anything. I know everyone has to learn, and it was an Experience."

CHAPTER SEVEN

Tess
Goes
Home

*I*t was, she found, an experience that lasted her well on into the next day. When she got up, for she refused to stay in bed for breakfast, although Mrs. Steadman herself came and tried to persuade her, she almost yelped with anguish as she stepped out of bed, and when she sat down for breakfast, her movements were unusually deliberate and dignified. Pat, Mrs. Steadman, and Jack, who could not forget her gallant efforts of the day before, were full of sympathy, but she had to put up with some teasing from Mr. Steadman and Uncle John before the meal was over. Billy, regarding her with no little scorn, said that Pinkie, although seriously injured, was not complaining at all.

But after a good night's sleep Tess had recovered her poise and took it all with smiling good humor. There was no question of a ride that day. Jack went off after breakfast, and Tess and Pat spent the day helping Mrs. Steadman. Tess, whose holidays at the seaside cottage had given her some experience in cooking, offered to make the pudding and a cake for tea.

"Oh, good," said Mrs. Steadman. "Will you? I'd be so glad. It's no good asking Pat. She's wonderful with children or animals, but she has a very heavy hand in the kitchen." So Tess put in a large part of the day by the big kitchen range. She was pleased to see that her cakes turned out all right and the pudding set as it should, but she was glad enough when she ripped off her apron and stepped out onto the veranda. It was hot outside in the middle of the afternoon, but the kitchen was an inferno, and her admiration for Mrs. Steadman increased enormously when she considered that she must spend a large part of every day in that broiling place. She compared it with her mother's compact, airy kitchen with its electric stove, and thought of the few bottles of milk that came in every morning, the neat parcels of chops, and the wrapped pounds of butter. Here Mrs. Steadman coped with buckets of milk, made her own butter from the separated cream, thinking herself remarkably lucky that she didn't have to do the separating too, and received enormous trays of mutton every few days to stack in the refrigerator. She was, in her own way, as competent and energetic as Mrs. Moorland and never showed any regret for her own neglected talent. Tess liked her very much.

Neither Pat nor Jack cared to suggest another ride on Dreadnaught, and they were surprised and pleased when Tess asked that night, before they went to bed, if she might try again the next day.

"Good girl," said Uncle John from beneath a mountain of newspapers, for the mail had just come in. "There's no better cure for stiffness. Tell you what, get Pat to bring you up to the stud farm again, and we'll demonstrate to this miserable unbeliever"—he indicated Jack—

"that you've got an eye as good as his for a beast. And that's not saying much," he added as an afterthought.

Tess was dismayed at this suggestion, but Uncle John waved away all objections. He was not accustomed, he said grandly, to having his plans objected to by serfs and underlings, and thus it would be.

So the next morning Pat and Tess set off on Dreadnaught and Turpin for the stud farm. Jack, to his intense disgust, had been commanded to accompany Uncle John in Geraldine, and they had roared off some time before in a cloud of dust and exhaust smoke. Silver raced along behind them, although Uncle John had offered to have him in the back seat.

"What?" said Jack in horror. "Risk a dog like Silver in Geraldine?"

This time Tess and Dreadnaught managed much more happily together. Her stiffness, agonizing when she first got on, wore off after a time, and she was able to enjoy the cool, sweet-smelling shade as they rode with muffled hoofs through a pine plantation. Once, to her delight, they saw a mob of about ten kangaroos hopping off through the blotched shadows of the pines.

"Sometimes there are so many," said Pat, "that they have to have kangaroo drives. It seems such a pity, but they can do a lot of damage."

As they rode on, Pat tried to explain to Tess how she could pick a good bull from a bad one. "You see, they're bred for beef," she said. "So they've got to have plenty of meat on them. They've got to be square and broad and solid, and the horns have to be flat and not round, because that means the other bones are flat, too, and better cuts come off a flat bone."

Tess listened carefully and tried to remember and understand, but it all sounded barbaric and complicated. She didn't like to think about those big, comfortable animals as so many sirloins, boned and rolled, or so much fillet steak. But she felt she must try to live up to the rather embarrassing "eye" that Uncle John insisted that she owned. She wondered vaguely which one it was. Was it slightly larger than the other? Or of a different shape, or color? "Bull's-eye," she suddenly thought, and chuckled.

When they arrived, Uncle John took them to a small paddock beside the yards. Under a tree in the corner stood half a dozen solid-looking red cows, each with a small red calf.

"There," said Uncle John. "We think we have next year's prizewinners among that lot. Now pick out the one you like best, Tess."

"Among the calves, do you mean?" asked Tess.

"Of course. Where else?" said Uncle John. "Have a good look at them now and just pick your fancy."

"How could she possibly pick them at that age?" asked Jack. "You can't tell how they'll develop."

"Because, my boy," said Uncle John impressively, "at that age you pick them by instinct, and we're going to test Tess out. I want you to try, too. You haven't any instinct, but you're shrewd, I'll grant you that. It's always interesting to try out a theory," he said, rather as if he had Tess and Jack in slides under a microscope.

So Tess accepted her fate and looked carefully at the calves. They were all about the same age and were as alike as peas in a pod. She felt inclined to shut her eyes and point, but decided it would be kinder to Uncle John to try to find some difference, however slight, among them. After a short time she pointed to one that stood

facing her, his eyes big with curiosity. He was strong
and healthy, and she was sure he looked more intelligent
than the others.

"I like him," she said, and would have tried to explain
why, but Uncle John held up his hand.

"No. That'll do," he said. "I don't want to know why.
Now he's"—he pulled out a little notebook and con-
sulted it—"ah, yes, 405. Quite likely. I incline to him
myself. You see?" he said, turning to Jack. "Not con-
clusive, of course. But straws in the wind, my boy. Now
you try."

"I'll pick Vanity's calf," said Jack promptly. "He's got
the breeding."

"Good, good," said Uncle John. "I'll mark him, too. A
sound reason, of course. But that's what I mean. Reason
isn't everything."

As no one was prepared to contradict him, he made
a mark in his notebook and slid it back into his pocket.
The test was over. After another brief look at the bulls
in the yards, Pat and Tess started for home. Uncle John
decided that as he had had the forethought to bring some
manpower with him, he might as well take some straw
back that Mrs. Steadman wanted for her hens' nests, and
the last they saw of Jack was a dogged figure forking
bundles of straw into the back seat. Uncle John, who
was talking to Johnson with an elbow on the fence, en-
couraged him with a cheerful word from time to time.
He was apparently preparing for a good twelve months'
frenzied laying on the part of the hens.

By this time, including the two days of the trip up, a
large part of Tess's holiday had already gone. They were
to take her into town to meet the plane the following
Sunday, and two days after that Pat and Jack would

have to leave for their respective boarding schools in not very distant country towns.

The next few days passed pleasantly for Tess. No more unexpected accidents befell her, and she was learning to accept the scorching heat, the dust, the flies, and the clouds of little singing mosquitoes that came with evening. They climbed up Sugarloaf, but it was not as difficult as she expected, and the view was, as Pat had promised, magnificent. Privately, Tess thought that this low, rolling country was inclined to be monotonous, but there was a sense of freedom and space about it that she enjoyed. Once they went for a picnic, and she got bitten by a greenhead ant. Frequently she had to extract clover burrs, the vicious seeds of khaki weed, or sharp grass seeds from among her clothes. There were plenty of small hazards and discomforts one way and another, but she was beginning to overcome them and to believe that someday, if she were given time to get used to it, she might really begin to enjoy country life. But on her final day something occurred that shattered all her confidence and made her glad, in spite of the fondness she had begun to feel for the Steadmans, that she was going home.

It happened just before lunch. The Steadman family was drifting, as was their habit, in ones and twos toward the dining room. Pat and Tess had come in from a ride, and while Tess went into the bathroom on the end of the veranda to wash her hands, Pat went up to the kitchen to see if she could help her mother, who was already serving the meal. Uncle John was strolling down the garden path from the yards, Mr. Steadman was talking on the telephone in the hall nearby, and Jack was sitting on the edge of the veranda, his small brother beside him, waiting for the approach of the traymobile from the kitchen.

On the side of the double part of the veranda where the kitchen building joined the main one stood a large dirty-linen basket not far from the kitchen door. As Pat passed it, she glanced down, gasped, and jumped quickly to one side. From the bathroom Tess heard her say, "Quick, Jack. Here's a snake." With practiced presence of mind, Pat stayed where she was and watched the snake while Jack jumped to his feet, scooped up Billy, and deposited him in the dining room, shutting the door behind him. Then he ran up the veranda, returning in record time with the garden rake. As soon as he arrived,

Pat darted into the kitchen and came out again almost immediately with the broom, which she held, bristles up, poised for action.

Tess, the towel still in her hands and her eyes popping, peered around the bathroom door. She had had no experience with snakes, and the thought of them made the hair at the back of her neck prickle. This one, she saw, was coiled comfortably around the washbasket, its little head low on the ground and the threadlike tongue flickering in and out. Just as Jack leaned over to lift up the basket, Uncle John arrived with a serviceable-looking piece of twisted wire. In spite of his large size he moved quietly and quickly. "Right," he said, bending his knees a little and lifting the wire. "Off with the basket, but look out you don't bring the snake with it." Jack, with one quick movement, twisted the basket up and out of the way. Pat lunged forward and banged with her broom, and Tess saw the snake writhe suddenly up the wall. As it came down, Uncle John struck, too, but the veranda boards here were rough, giving a hold to its scales, and it twisted quickly, trying to get away into the piece of garden between the kitchen and the bathroom. But Jack hit out with his rake, and though he missed it, he managed to turn it back again onto the veranda. And now Tess saw, to her horror, that it was coming in a series of fluid curves that made a dry, slithering sound on the boards, straight toward her. Pat and Uncle John raced down after it, and she had a confused impression of thudding feet, bangs and bumps and darting figures, cheers and shrieks of excitement from the dining room, and ahead of it all the thin, dull brown twisting body of the snake, its little head half an inch off the ground, flying for its life. As it drew near, she stepped back hurriedly into the bathroom. But the snake was trying to get away to the left to the safety of the garden, and until it reached the bathroom, it had found Jack and his rake waiting whenever it tried to twist around. Now, the open door of the bathroom offered protection. Before any of them quite realized what had happened, it dived in after Tess.

"Look out, Tess!" Jack called.

But Uncle John said in a quiet voice that somehow they all heard, "Stand quite still, everybody." He put his hand on Pat's arm as she was about to rush through the door. Then, his eyes on the floor, he went softly to the bathroom. "Are you all right, Tess?" he asked.

A whisper answered him. "Yes, but it's here, on the floor—beside the bath."

"Good," replied Uncle John. "Stand quite still then. I'll have him fixed in a jiffy. I don't think he can get a grip on that slippery linoleum." He turned to Pat and Jack. "Watch now, in case he tries to come out." He leaned forward and slowly pushed the door farther open. They saw Tess standing rigid, pressed against the washbasin, her face white and her eyes fixed on something they couldn't see behind the door. Uncle John grasped his wire and stepped softly through the door, backing up against the wall as he got inside. The door closed, and Pat and Jack waited outside, watching the half-inch gap under it. For a moment there was silence; then there came two sharp cracks, a scuffle of feet, and Uncle John's voice.

"Now hop up onto the edge of the bath, Tess, like a good girl. You'll be out of my way." There came three or four more cracks, one after the other, and then Uncle John spoke again in an amiable conversational tone.

"That's fixed him, I think. You can come down now." The door opened, and he emerged with the still twisting body of the snake hanging from his wire.

"All over," he said. "You can go and have dinner now. I'll just drop this into the furnace." He walked off around the corner of the bathroom, and Tess, looking a little uncertain and still white about the mouth, came out onto the veranda.

"Tess!" said Pat, going up to her and putting a hand on her arm. "Are you all right?"

"I believe I am," said Tess, rather in the manner of a sleepwalker. "It was—it was rather exciting, though, for a few minutes there."

"I'll bet it was," said Jack with feeling. "I had no idea the thing would try that, or I'd have warned you. It's the first time we've ever had a snake in the bathroom, isn't it, Pat?"

"I think it is," said Pat thoughtfully. "We've had a few in the hall, one in the sitting room once, and there was that time Mum found one under her bed, but never in the bathroom."

"Oh," said Tess, and giggled a little wildly. "I did think it could have been called an Experience, but it seems to be all in the day's work. I never dreamed things like this happened with such tedious monotony."

Jack grinned. "Well, it's not quite like that, though we do have a few snakes about in the summer as a rule. But we're not in the habit of shutting them up with our guests. I think—yes, I really think you might class this as an Experience."

At that moment Mr. Steadman's head came around the hall door. "What in the name of heaven has been going on here?" he asked. "I've been trying to get a long distance call, and the pandemonium out here made it almost impossible. Have you been doing folk dances or something?"

"They found a snake, I think," said Mrs. Steadman's voice calmly from the kitchen. "I was just doing the scones, so I couldn't see." She looked around the screen door. "Did you get it, dear?" she asked.

Pat and Jack, both speaking together, gave them a confused but exciting account of what had happened.

"Oh, poor Tess," said Mrs. Steadman when they had finished. "What a nasty experience! I'm so glad it didn't bite you."

But Mr. Steadman was not even faintly amused. "What on earth were you thinking of," he said to Jack, "to let Tess get mixed up in it? You ought to have had more sense."

Jack was saved the necessity of a reply by Uncle John's appearance. He was rubbing his hands with satisfaction.

"A neat bit of work," he remarked. "Of course the poor thing was practically helpless on that slippery floor, but nevertheless it had its moments, didn't it, Tess?"

"It did," said Tess.

"Have you been hearing the thrilling story, Bob?" he asked his brother.

"I heard enough of it," said Mr. Steadman, "to wonder what on earth you were all thinking of to involve Tess in it."

Uncle John's eyebrows rose. "My dear fellow, it was entirely unpremeditated, I assure you. We thought Tess was well out of the way. To be honest, I never saw her at all. How were we to know the snake possessed an odd passion for bathrooms? Last thing I ever expected."

Mr. Steadman's frown relaxed. "Oh, well," he said, "no damage done, I expect."

"Except that poor Tess has had a nasty shock, and on an empty stomach, too," said Mrs. Steadman. "It's time we all had some lunch. Go in, all of you, while I bring it in."

And that was, perhaps, the most vivid memory that Tess took away with her when she left Pillana the following day. She was very sorry to say good-bye to the Steadmans, and she knew that she was leaving behind a number of things that she would miss, but she felt, just as Jack had felt after his accident in the lake, that she did not know enough of this sort of life to be entirely at home in it yet. There was a certain relief to be returning to a life she understood, to a place where the heat was not so fierce, where flies did not rush to sit on you the minute you went out of the door, and where snakes did not bail you up in bathrooms.

Mr. Steadman and Pat drove her into town, and not long before they reached the airstrip, Pat said, "You'll fly right over the top of the Karkoo Ranges. You should have a wonderful view of Calca. Do write and tell me what it's like."

"And think of them," added Mr. Steadman, "perched on top of it next September, stiff and tired and sore from sleeping on damp ground."

"It sounds wonderful," said Tess, for whom new ventures always had a charm. "I do wish I were coming with you."

Pat clasped her hands and swung around. "Why don't you?" she asked. "Do come! It would be wonderful. Could you? Possibly?"

Tess's eyes lit up. Gone were the memories of flies, dust, grass seeds, and snakes. Here was an adventure, an Experience! "I'd simply love to," she said on a deep breath.

"It will be darned uncomfortable, remember that," warned Mr. Steadman.

"Oh, but it will be glorious," said Pat. "Think of the packhorses and the campfires. Can you really come?"

"Are you sure I wouldn't be a nuisance?" asked Tess.

"Of course you won't be," said Pat. "It would be much more fun if you came, too."

"I'll see if I can manage it then," said Tess, her eyes gleaming with excitement. "I'll talk to Mother and write and let you know."

They passed through Talia and out about a mile and a half to the airstrip. The plane was waiting, shining in the morning sun. Tess said good-bye and climbed aboard. Just before she dived inside, she stopped and turned.

"See you in September—I hope," she said, and around her smiling face even the dark curls seemed to crackle and snap with excitement.

They waited while the plane roared and vibrated into life, raising a cloud of dust with its whirling propellers. It taxied to the end of the strip, turned, and moved slowly forward, increasing speed until, a long way from them, they saw it leave the ground and soar into the blue summer sky. When it had height enough, it turned, headed for Sydney, and grew small. The sound died away, and Tess, high above, returned to her home and to the beginning of the term.

CHAPTER EIGHT

Preparing for Calca

But Pat, when she returned to Pillana and told Jack that Tess hoped to climb Calca with them in September, found herself in trouble.

"Do you mean to say you asked Tess to come with us?" said Jack.

"Yes," said Pat. "And she's dying to come. She's going to ask her mother and let me know. You don't mind, do you?"

"Mind?" said Jack, and seemed to run out of words. After a pause while he battled with his feelings, he said with resigned disgust, "It'll ruin the whole thing, that's all."

"But I thought you liked Tess now," said Pat, and remembered, too late, that she had made this mistake before.

"Well, so I do," said Jack. "She's not a bad kid. But you know what she's like up here. We'll have to spend all our time nursemaiding her. Oh, Pat, whyever did you do it?"

"Oh, dear," said Pat miserably. "I'm awfully sorry. I thought she'd like it, and it would be fun for me, and I didn't think you'd mind a bit."

"It's not that so much," said Jack with deep gloom, "but think of Mick and Dick Felton. What do you think they're going to say when I tell them we're dragging a city girl along?"

"I don't see what the Feltons have got to do with it," said Pat in bewilderment.

"But I *told* you," Jack fairly shouted. "We're going to spend the night on their place and go up the Karkoos from there. They're almost at the foot of the mountains."

"I know," said Pat. "But you never said Mick and Dick were coming with us."

"Well, I meant to," said Jack, as if that were sufficient. "Because they are. It was really almost their idea when we first talked it over at school. They'll probably want to put the whole thing off now when I tell them what's happened," he added in tones of the deepest dejection.

Mrs. Steadman, who had been sitting behind them in the big cane chair, her sketchbook on her lap, now spoke. "I don't think they will, Jack. It can't make so much difference to them. And to tell you the truth, I should be a good deal happier about this expedition if I thought Tess were going with you." Jack looked at his mother in surprise.

"I didn't think you were worried about it, Mother," he said.

"I know you didn't," said Mrs. Steadman. "And I wasn't going to spoil your fun. But I have been a little disturbed about Pat's going all that way with only you three boys."

"But you know we'd have looked after her," said Jack.

"I know you would have done your best, and I'm still sure you will. And I know Pat doesn't need much looking after. But all the same, I should like to think she had Tess with her. It will mean she needn't exhaust herself trying to do everything you boys want to do. I think you'll find it's not such a bad idea after all." She smiled at him and picked up her pencil.

"Oh," said Jack thoughtfully, and then, after a few minutes while Pat watched him anxiously, "well, I'd rather Tess came than we left Pat behind. I'll tell Mick and Dick when I see them next week. I needn't tell them she's a city girl," he ended hopefully.

Pat's round, sunburned face broke into a wide smile of relief. "Oh, *thank* you, Jack," she said with such humble gratitude that Jack smiled, too.

She wondered often during the next few months when she was back at school whether Jack had told the Feltons and whether, as he had prophesied, they had immediately called off the whole scheme. Jack never wrote to her when they were at school, and she did not expect a letter, but she often thought of the Karkoo expedition and could hardly wait until she saw Jack again in the May holidays. Halfway through the term she had a letter from Tess, forwarded by her mother from Pillana. It said that Tess had asked Mrs. Moorland if she could go, and Mrs. Moorland had said if she was sure she wanted to spend her holiday in such an odd way she might, though she didn't see why it was necessary to go all that way to sleep on the ground when she could do it much more simply down at the seaside. Mrs. Moorland, said Tess, had a kindergarten conference in September and would really be glad to have her out of the way. As for Mary, she was already talking of buying

Tess camp beds, valises, collapsible baths, tents, and anything else collapsible she could think of, for she was sure she would never see her young sister again and wished to make her end as comfortable as possible.

Pat was pleased, but her pleasure was mixed with doubt, and it was not until she saw Jack again and he told her that the Feltons had raised no objection that she allowed herself to look forward with anything like real excitement to the adventure.

"I'm so glad they didn't mind," she said when he told her.

"So am I," said Jack. "As a matter of fact, they said they had supposed all the time that you would have a mate."

"Oh," said Pat, "if we'd only known."

"I know," said Jack. "I'm sorry I got so cranky. I'm used to the idea now, but somehow I never associated Tess with Calca, and it did seem pretty awful at first."

"She'll be all right," said Pat confidently.

They spent a large part of the May holidays sorting out the gear they intended to take with them. It was not strictly necessary, for they would have at least a week at home in September before the expedition. But Jack and the Feltons appeared to have devoted most of their previous term's studies to the articles considered indispensable to mountaineers, explorers, and others and had made exhaustive lists, all of which had eventually been scrapped in favor of one that agreed more nearly with the boys' own previous camping experience. This, considering it catered for all the needs of six people for a period of nearly a week, was commendably brief.

Even so, when Pat had read through, she pointed to

an item with her finger. "Twenty-four pounds of butter seems an awful lot," she said.

"Is it?" said Jack. "Mick said you'd see the practical side. He says girls are always useful when it comes to tucker and quantities. But are you sure it's too much? One eats an awful lot of butter, you know."

"Well, if we eat as much as this, we'll all be sick," said Pat. And she altered the item with her pencil.

After one or two more additions and discardings, they gave the list to Mr. Steadman for a final check. He studied it carefully and then looked up. "There are only two things I might suggest: a billy and some matches."

"Good grief!" said Jack. "Did we forget those?"

"I don't see them here," said Mr. Steadman. "It's always the obvious things like that one does forget."

In the end they decided on a list that even Mr. Steadman agreed would be adequate but not too extensive. Jack took it back to school to be divided between themselves and the Feltons.

It only remained to wait with what patience they could for the next holidays. The midwinter term wore itself on. Jack and the two Felton boys had frequent discussions on their plan of campaign, and Pat amused herself writing to Tess every time she thought of something else Tess ought to bring with her. And Tess, who went to a day school, would add one or two more things to her suitcase every time she received Pat's letter. They thought that the spring would never come, but little by little the nights became shorter, the days became warmer, and eventually, for them all, the term ended. The Felton boys went off to their home by the Karkoo Ranges, Pat and Jack took their respective trains to Talia, and Tess flung the last few things into her now bulging suitcase and banged down the lid. She said good-bye to her mother, who told her absentmindedly not to get her feet wet, and to Mary, who asked her to be sure to leave the address of her next of kin at Pillana, and stepped aboard the Northwest Mail.

At noon the following day Pat, Jack, and Silver met her at the Talia railway station. She was touched when Silver caressed her hand with a wet nose and gently waved his tail.

"He remembers me," she said in surprise.

"Of course he does," said Jack. "But he doesn't often do that to anyone but the family."

From that moment Tess was Silver's devoted admirer.

They extracted her suitcase from the baggage car, and in a few minutes she found herself climbing into Geraldine with more pleasure than she had ever done before.

"I'm sorry we couldn't meet you in style," said Jack. "But the roads are a bit sticky, and Geraldine has a way with her in the mud that the car hasn't."

They picked up Mrs. Steadman and a large number of parcels at the general store and called at the drugstore and the grocery for more parcels before they turned off Talia's main street and headed for Pillana. They all had a great deal to say and covered the distance so quickly, it seemed to Tess, that she asked if they had come home a shorter way.

She saw again the wide plain, the clustered trees of the homestead, and the sprawling stockyards beside it, and wondered that it all seemed so familiar and so homelike.

As they walked up the veranda, laden with parcels

and bulging paper bags, Uncle John came out to meet them.

"Very glad to see you back, Tess," he said, smiling. "I was sure you'd never set foot on Pillana again after your last adventure here."

"I know," said Tess, and her face became slightly pink as she remembered that she had thought the same. "But I'm dying to climb the mountain with them, and I didn't think being shut in a bathroom with a snake was a thing that could happen regularly—even here."

"Good gracious, I should hope not," said Mrs. Steadman, quite shocked at the thought.

"Unlikely," said Uncle John. Then his eye traveled over the multitude of packages. "Don't tell me that Jack has been sending you some of his lists," he said to Tess. "Are all these yours? Did they tell you to bring all this stuff?"

"Of course it isn't, John," said Mrs. Steadman. "What on earth would Tess be doing with two dozen packets of bluing, or all those bananas? Come along, children. Drop the parcels and come in to lunch. Same room, Tess, but not the best sheets. You're one of the family now."

Pat took Tess to her room but stopped suddenly in the doorway. "Oh, dear," she said.

Tess, looking over her shoulder, saw that the cover of her bed had been turned down, and on the pillow, more grubby and battered than ever, sat Pinkie. He wore a large and brightly colored tie, and around his head, hooked over one ear, was a crown of twisted tie-wire.

"He's a princess now," explained Pat. "That's why he wears the crown. But I don't know what he's doing in here." She went over to pick him up, but Tess stopped her.

"Better leave him till we find out," she said. "It might be a gesture, and it would be a pity to spoil it."

"But he's so dirty," said Pat. "If you knew the places he gets to—"

"Well, don't tell me," said Tess quickly. "If I don't know, I shan't mind. We'll ask Billy."

Mr. Steadman and Billy came in after the others had started lunch. They had spent the morning at the wool-shed.

"Nice to see you again, Tess," said Mr. Steadman as he sat down. "But don't say afterward that I didn't warn you."

Before going to his seat, Billy walked up to Tess.

"Pinkie's a princess now," he said. "You'll find her in your bed. You can have him to sleep with while you're here. She won't mind." And, scowling slightly, he turned and marched back to his own chair.

"Thank you very much," said Tess, rising to the occasion. "If you're sure you won't miss him, I should love to have her."

Tess found that this time she fitted very easily and happily into the daily routine of the Steadman family. She knew her way about, and she was treated, as Mrs. Steadman had told her she would be, as one of themselves. Once or twice she and Pat went out riding, for shearing was not quite finished and there were sheep to be moved. She still rode Dreadnaught, but she felt that they understood one another better now. Also, the sun, which she had felt to be an enemy on those first summer days, now shone with a gentle warmth in the crisp spring air. Gone were the small flies, the mosquitoes, and the dust; and the long plains beneath the great arch of the sky were preparing secretly for the summer growth of grass and herbage. There was an exhilaration in the air that Tess felt, but could not yet, and did not try to, understand.

For the first few days they made no preparations for the trip. Jack and his Silver were out all the daylight hours, and Pat and Tess paid several visits to the wool-shed.

The big corrugated-iron building had come to life. It was surrounded now by a sea of sheep, some yards full of woolly ones, round, comfortable, and yellowish gray from twelve months of weather and dust, other yards full of shorn sheep, slim, snow-white with occasional flecks of bright red where the shears had gone too close, more agile, but lost and bewildered among creatures they no longer recognized as themselves. Inside, the shed was full of men and boys and wool. Down one side, each at his own stand, stood the shearers, bending, turning, and twisting as they slid the handpieces in long, rhythmic sweeps over the prostrate sheep. The fleeces rolled off like blankets, and every so often a shearer would push his shorn sheep down a chute to the yard outside, straighten himself for a moment, and then reach into the pen beside him for the next victim. Boys raced with the fleeces from the shearing stands to the wool tables and then turned to sprint for the next. On the tables the fleeces were pounced on by men who stripped them of their ragged edges, rolled them in creamy, fluffy bundles, and took them over to the wool classer.

Pat pointed out the classer to Tess. "That's Mr. Richards," she said. "He comes to us every year, and Father and Uncle John say he's very good."

Tess looked with interest at Mr. Richards. He was a small middle-aged man who worked at his table with a

kind of dreamy concentration, a cigarette in the corner
of his mouth. He seemed unaware of the hurly-burly
around him and behaved rather as if he were the high
priest of this hectic annual ritual. Behind him was a row
of large wooden bins built like cages; and each con-
tained, according to its grade, a mounting pile of fleeces.

Around and among all this central activity were boys
with brooms, boys with tar brushes, and men dragging
huge baskets of wool across the floor, while behind them
all and near the main entrance was the wool press, a
huge boxlike affair, worked by the biggest man Tess had
ever seen. He was naked to the waist, and all over him,
even clinging to the stubble on his chin, were little tufts
of wool. Beside the press stood the finished bales of
wool, stenciled and ready for the trucks that would take
them to the nearest rail siding. Above the multitude of
sounds came the steady throb of the engine that drove
the shearing machines, and permeating everything was
the pungent, pleasant smell of sheep and wool.

Tess absorbed it all and found it strangely exciting.

"And does this happen every year?" she asked Pat.

Pat smiled and nodded. "Yes, it's fun, isn't it?"

"It's terrific," said Tess.

Going home that day, they stopped to watch Jack and
Silver taking away a mob of shorn sheep. As usual, Silver
was doing all the work. He seemed to know exactly
where they were to go and how to get them there. He
raced from one side to the other, silent except when he
gave a short bark that would send a straggler back to
the mob. It was quite obvious that he was enjoying
himself.

"I'm not surprised Jack thinks so much of him," said
Tess. "Are all sheep dogs as good as that?"

"Not many," said Pat. "They're like people, you know. Some are good and some are bad, and some have brains and some haven't. But Silver's extra good. Jack wouldn't part with him for anything. He was a Christmas present from Father a few years ago, and now I think Father wishes he'd kept him for himself."

"I suppose Mr. Steadman uses him while Jack's at school," said Tess. But Pat shook her head.

"He won't work for anyone but Jack. Border collies are like that, they say."

By the time shearing was over, they found that they had three days to get ready. On the fourth day they were to leave for the Karkoo Ranges.

"I suppose you'll be wanting Geraldine," said Uncle John regretfully.

"Well, we'd rather not have Geraldine, Uncle John, thanks all the same," said Jack, perhaps a shade too promptly, for Uncle John's eyebrows rose.

"Oh?" he said. "And what is wrong with Geraldine?"

Jack grinned. "It's just that she's a bit too slow. It would take us ages to get there."

"In the hands of a good driver, Geraldine goes like the wind," said Uncle John simply.

"As a matter of fact," said Mr. Steadman, "with the stuff they have to take, they wouldn't have a hope of fitting into Geraldine. They'll have to take the utility."

They settled down to the business of collecting their gear. Jack took one list, Pat another, and they marked off a corner of the veranda as a receiving depot. Food was to go in one place, blankets in another, cooking utensils and miscellaneous articles elsewhere; it was all very methodical and efficient. But, as in all things, the human element was apt to upset the nicest calculations. Jack would decide that the pile of blankets was far too big and remove one or two while Pat was absent; Pat would look with horror at the growing mound of sardines, tinned fruit, and packets of biscuits and hurry back to the kitchen with an armful that she felt sure would be unnecessary. And each, coming back to his own pile, would find that it had been tampered with. There would be questions, explanations, reproaches, and they would be obliged to hold yet another conference, and the lists would be amended yet again. Or sometimes Billy, with bright-eyed enthusiasm, would offer to help, and it seemed unkind to stop him. But afterward it would be necessary to extract a remarkable assortment of articles from the pile; after one bout of assistance Tess found herself returning to the house with the fire tongs, a wastepaper basket, and a hearthrug decorated with pink roses. And this had to be done with tact and discretion so that feelings would not be wounded. Pinkie, too, had a habit of getting mixed up with the provisions, for he had an urgent desire, so Billy told them, of joining the expedition, and no matter how often they removed him, he found his way back again. And Silver, entering into the spirit of the thing, would follow Jack around the veranda, trailing a pullover or an odd sock that he had salvaged from the pile of Jack's belongings. Jack received them all gratefully and in due course returned them.

Eventually, however, all was ready. Jack spent the last morning filling the utility with gas and checking the water, oil, and tires. Tess, watching him, suddenly said, "Will it be all right, your driving all that way without a license?"

Jack raised his head from the engine and looked at her. "A fellow doesn't stay sixteen forever, you know," he said reproachfully.

"Oh," said Tess as light dawned. "Have you really gotten your license now? How wonderful!" And at the admiration in her tone he grinned.

"Got it a month ago as a matter of fact," he said.

In the afternoon they packed their stuff into the utility. There was not much room to spare, but Pat noticed that Jack was very carefully leaving one corner free.

At last she said, "For goodness' sake put something in that corner, or the things will slide about."

He shook his head. "Can't," he said. "Silver's got to have somewhere to sit, and you know we can't have him in front because he gets sick."

"Silver?" Pat almost shrieked. "Is he coming?"

"He is," said Jack firmly. "Any objection?"

"Oh, no," said Pat mildly. "I was just surprised."

"It'll be good training for him," said Jack.

Afterward Tess said to Pat, "What sort of training would a sheep dog get up in those hills?" But Pat smiled.

"He just likes to have Silver with him," she said. "But he doesn't want to say so. I hope," she added, "that Silver isn't too carsick."

That night they went to bed early, and as Tess switched off her light, wriggled herself down, and tucked the sheet under her chin, she felt a tingle of excitement along her spine. "An Experience," she thought happily, her eyes wide in the darkness. The outline of the window became luminous, and she could see faintly the shape of a tree in the garden. One or two stars pricked the night, and there was no sound at all, not even a mopoke. She remembered how the complete silence of the night had disturbed her at first. She had felt that at any moment it must be shattered, and she would lie awake, waiting for the crash of sound her ears expected. But it never came, and now she accepted the silence gratefully as part of the new life she was learning to understand. She sighed, her foot twitched suddenly, and in a few moments her breathing slowed to the long rhythm of sleep.

CHAPTER NINE

Prelude

*T*he next morning Pat, as usual, was awake first. She burst into Tess's room on her way to the shower. Her eyes were bright and the bleached hair wild about her head.

"This is it," she said as Tess rolled over. "Jack says we're to start straight after breakfast." And she vanished toward the bathroom. As Tess slithered out of bed, she heard an unusual sound. Above the splashing of the shower, Pat was singing. It was a tuneless song but very happy. Tess made her bed quickly, flung the last few things into the kit bag that Jack had allowed her as personal luggage, and followed Pat to the shower.

For once no one was late for breakfast. It was true that Billy had failed to do up any buttons and his shoelaces trailed, but he had a handicap of so many years, and to be in time for breakfast made up for many shortcomings. Mr. Steadman, passing around scrambled eggs, regarded the adventurers thoughtfully.

"Everything packed?" he asked at last.

"All stowed but the toothbrushes," said Jack. "Any final instructions?"

"I think not," said Mr. Steadman. "Drive carefully, that's all. And don't let those young Feltons put too many crazy ideas into your heads."

"Of course not," said Jack. "Everything's worked out to the last decimal point, anyway."

"And we're taking exactly what was on the lists you and Uncle John checked with us—nothing else at all," said Pat.

A strange noise, half-hoot, half-cackle, came from Billy. But when they looked at him, his eyes were wide and limpid, and he smiled angelically. Only his cheeks were faintly pink.

"Anything wrong?" asked Jack. But Billy shook his head and attended to his scrambled egg with ferocity.

"I rang Mrs. Felton yesterday," said Mrs. Steadman, the milk jug in her hand. "Not that I wanted to interfere, but as you'll be her guests tonight, I thought I'd better. She says she's expecting you sometime this afternoon, and everything's arranged for tomorrow."

"Oh, good!" said Pat. "How lovely! To think it's really come at last." Her face was a moon of joy as she gazed around the table at her family.

After breakfast the girls ran off to get their kit bags and coats, and the rest of the family left the wreck of the breakfast table without a second thought and made their way to the utility. Jack came up with Silver, flat-eared and joyfully squirming, and shortly afterward Pat and Tess arrived and handed him their luggage. He climbed onto the back and stowed the kit bags carefully.

"All set now," he said, jumping down. "Hop in, Silver." The dog scrambled over the tailboard and sat down in his corner, panting happily. They said good-bye with the emphasis and finality that Christopher Columbus must have used when parting from his dear ones long ago in Genoa, and Pat opened the door of the utility. Jack started around to the driving side, but stopped suddenly.

"Christmas!" he said. "I've forgotten to bring any bones for Silver." There was a dismayed pause, then, with one accord, Mrs. Steadman, Pat, and Billy raced for the kitchen. The others waited, tongue-tied, in that brief sample of eternity between the farewell and the departure.

"Sure you haven't forgotten anything?" said Mr. Steadman belatedly.

"Only a few old bones," said Tess with a giggle, and the moment was past.

"Make sure they look after you," said Mr. Steadman, smiling at her. "You'll find it a bit rough up there."

"She can take it," said Jack with a confidence that made Tess glow with pleasure.

A shuffling and bumping announced the return of the others, and Billy appeared around the corner of the veranda dragging a sugar bag.

"That's all we can find," said Mrs. Steadman behind him. "If it's not enough, he'll have to eat your rations."

"There's a nice lot of meat on some of them," said Pat with satisfaction, "and beautifully ripe."

In another minute they were aboard, Jack started up the engine, and they were off.

They rumbled over the ramp, turned onto the track across the plain, and headed for Talia—and the Karkoo Ranges. Tess heaved a sigh of content and wriggled herself comfortable. The morning air still tingled, but the sun, in a cloudless sky, poured its warmth on the earth.

By lunchtime they had reached the dead flat plains that Tess remembered from her former journey. The spring had transformed them to a velvet green, very different from the scorched and glaring parchment of late summer. The season was further advanced here, and at midday the sun was hot. They lunched off sandwiches, hard-boiled eggs, and Thermos tea in the tarry-smelling shade of a pine plantation.

"Tell me about the Feltons," said Tess, digging her heels into the pine needles.

"Nothing much to tell, really," said Jack. "They live on a small place just outside the town. Mr. Felton had something to do with some properties in the Far West, but he's sort of retired, and he doesn't do much here but just potter. He's quite a nice old boy. There are only the two boys, Mick and Dick."

"How old are they?" asked Tess.

"Dick's sixteen; Mick's thirteen, but they seem to think he's a bit of a brain at school. He's always the baby of his form."

"Have they got a mother?" said Tess, determined to have them firmly fixed before she met them.

"Mrs. Felton? Oh, yes," said Jack in surprise. "Didn't you hear Mother say she rang her up yesterday? She always looks as if she's going to a party. Mick and Dick are terribly proud of her. And I must say," he went on magnanimously, "she is one of the school's most presentable mothers. You'd be surprised how some get themselves up."

But Tess shook her head vigorously. "I wouldn't," she said. "Not after what we sometimes see on the beach."

"Us, for instance," said Pat with a glance at Jack.

"Oh, no, not you," said Tess, horrified. "You were all most respectable. We spotted you at once for some of the nice ones. Of course we could see you weren't used to the beach. But that didn't stop your being nice, did it? We were dying to give you a hand."

"Were you really?" said Jack, struck by this point of view. "We thought—I thought—" he amended honestly, "you were rather superior."

"Oh, Jack," said Pat. But Tess laughed.

"That's because we were at home there, I expect. And I felt just the same when I first came up here. I thought I'd never learn."

"And we all were wrong, then," said Jack. "Come on, we'd better get going again if you've both finished." He got to his feet and stretched. "Just the right weather for camping. We should be able to see the ranges in another half-hour."

They packed up the lunch quickly and set off again. Silver, whose high spirits had noticeably evaporated by lunchtime, had recovered and was only anxious that he should not be left behind.

Late in the afternoon they passed through the main street of Kullaroo, which was the Feltons' town and the nearest of any size to the ranges. And just before sunset, having made one false start down a wrong road, they turned in at the main gate of the Feltons' property. They could see the house about half a mile away on a gentle slope facing east toward a small creek. It was not a large house, but it looked old and solid and was backed by a number of big, shady trees. Behind it were a few small sheds, a set of sheepyards, and a woolshed about a quar-

ter of the size of the one at Pillana. The telephone and
electric lines kept them company along the track to the
homestead.

The track led around a smallish garden, full of spring
flowers, to the back of the house. As Jack stopped the
utility, two figures erupted from a door at the side and
raced across to them. "Hello, there!" shouted the first to
reach the gate. "Glad to see you made it all right. Mother
was sure you'd get bogged."

"Bogged?" said Jack. "There's been no rain, has there?"

"No, dry as a bone," said the young Felton. "But
Mother thinks everyone gets bogged. Don't bother to
tell me which is your sister. I can guess." An alert face
under a head of shining fair hair was thrust through
the window. Pat found herself scrutinized by a pair of
very blue, wide-open eyes.

"Right first time," said Jack. "This is Pat. And that dark
one there, that you don't seem to have noticed, is Tess
Moorland. This is Dick," he added as an afterthought to
the girls.

"Tess," said Dick, turning his attention to her. "What
a coincidence. I once had an old dog called Tess—the
best dog I ever had. I'm very pleased to know you."

Tess returned his gaze placidly. "I'll do my best to
justify the name," she murmured.

Dick laughed and wrenched open the door. "Can't go
wrong with a name like that," he said. "Come on.
Mother's waiting for you."

As they got out, they came face to face with the second
Felton. He was not as tall as his brother and less solidly
built. His hair, too, was darker and gathered itself into
an uncombed mop on top of his high forehead, giving

him a permanent air of surprise. He stood quietly, watching them as they sorted themselves out. Then, as they turned for the house, he said, "I'm Mick. How do you do."

Pat smiled her warm smile at him. "Of course, we knew you were Mick," she said. "Aren't we rude?"

"Oh, no," he said. "But now, you see, we're on speaking terms."

Dick led the way in, but Jack dropped behind to say to Mick, "A terrible thing it would be if you weren't able to speak."

"It is," said Mick slowly. "Happens every day, too—twice."

"I can't believe it," said Jack. "Not you."

"Fact," said Mick, looking earnestly at Jack. "M'mother's fault. Makes me clean my teeth twice a day."

Jack laughed, and they moved on after the others. A little farther on Mick said, as if he had been giving the matter considerable thought, "Er—not leaving your dog in the truck all night, are you?"

"Christmas! I forgot all about him," said Jack.

"Thought so," said Mick mildly.

Jack gave one shrill whistle, and in a second Silver was beside them. This time he presented Jack with a large, brightly colored sun hat that Tess had flung into the back as she left the utility a few moments before. Mick's eyes widened when he saw it.

"Didn't know you went in for that kind of thing in the holidays. Must catch the wind a bit, riding about, doesn't it?" And once again Jack found it necessary to explain the singular accomplishment of his dog.

Mick regarded Silver with interest. "Seems a pity we can't take him inside with us," he said. "He'd probably be happier sitting up at table with a knife and fork. But Mother doesn't care for them in the house. 'Fraid he'll have to make do with the veranda." They hurried along to catch up with the others.

As Dick opened the door, he called, "Here they are, Mother. Got bogged right at our front gate."

They heard an exclamation of dismay, and then Mrs. Felton appeared. Tess saw at once that Jack's description —"always looks as if she's going to a party"—was exactly right. She was small and neat, and her gray hair curled crisply and tidily around her head. Her eyes were very bright, and above the frilled collar of her blue linen dress her face had an air of gaiety and good humor.

"You poor things!" she said, and then caught sight of Dick's broad smile. "You horrid boy. Of course they didn't. Just after Father put four truckloads of gravel there, too." She turned to them again. "He's always saying things like that, and I always believe him. I never seem to learn. Now come along. I'm sure you're tired and hungry, and dirty, too, I daresay, after that terrible road. I'll show you where you're sleeping, and Dick can tell me which of you is which as we go along. But don't tell me which Jack is because naturally I can see at a glance. Besides, I've met him before." She turned, so that they nearly bumped into her, to give Jack a flashing smile.

Dick snatched the moment's pause to say, "It's quite easy; the fair one is Pat, Jack's sister, and the dark one is Tess. Remember old Tess, Mother? Same name, so that makes it easy for you."

"Oh, doesn't it?" said Mrs. Felton, delighted. "That'll make us feel we know you *very* well."

She opened the door into a small room that was remarkable chiefly for a tumbling sea of cretonne material that lay about on the furniture. Two stretcher beds were jammed together at one end.

"The boys said I wasn't to make you too comfortable so the shock wouldn't be too great tomorrow. That's why you're in here among the new curtains. You're sure they won't give you nightmares?" she asked Pat anxiously.

"It will be lovely, thank you, Mrs. Felton," said Pat. "We'll be very careful not to disturb them."

"Oh, don't worry about them," said Mrs. Felton. "So long as you're comfortable—but not too comfortable, of course. The bathroom's just around the corner there. I'll leave you to have a wash, or a bath if you'd rather. Jack's on the veranda with the boys, and he can dress in their room." She went off with light steps, and Pat and Tess began to make themselves tidy.

Later, when they went into the sitting room, they found it occupied by a large, round-faced elderly gentleman. He was leaning well back, with his legs stretched out, in a big easy chair. He held a drink in one hand and was doing his best to control a newspaper with the other. As they came in, he raised his head and made a brief effort to get up, but sank back again with a sigh.

"You must excuse me," he said. "It's ten minutes' work for me to get out of this chair, but I'll introduce myself and you can do the same. I'm Dick and Mick's father."

"How do you do, Mr. Felton," said Pat. "I'm Pat, and this is Tess. It's awfully nice of you to have us all for the night."

"Not at all," he said amiably. "M' wife and I feel it's quite an honor to be able to participate in your adventure, even in this humble way. The boys have talked of nothing else, you know, for the past two holidays. What do you feel about it? Excited? Or perhaps a bit doubtful? I believe your—er—Tess—funny, we had a dog once called Tess—is from the city. A bit of an experience for you, isn't it?" he asked, rolling a curious eye at Tess.

"It will be," said Tess. "But I'm terribly pleased to be going."

He nodded comfortably. "Naturally; at your age, if you're worth anything, you would be. And you won't regret it, even if it is a bit rough. Sit down now. There's nothing to do in the kitchen. Your turn will come afterward, and m' wife will be in in a minute. The boys are putting your truck away."

They sat down, and he proceeded to talk to them in a meditative and friendly way until Mrs. Felton put her head around the door. "Oh, you've met," she said. "Good. Now come along because dinner's ready, and the boys have just come in. Let me give you a hand, Hugh." She went up to him and held out her hands, but he chuckled and shook his head.

"No good, m' dear. You know quite well you only end up flat on your face." He put down his glass and the paper, rested his palms on the arms of the chair, and struggled to his feet. Mrs. Felton watched him solicitously and then turned to the girls.

"He likes to pretend I'm a frail little old lady, but really I'm one of those who doesn't know their own strength." She led the way into the dining room. The boys were already there, and Mr. Felton sat himself down in front of a large leg of mutton.

"I suppose you people eat beef at this time of year," he said as he plunged the carving knife into the joint.

"We did once, too—out west," said Dick a little wistfully.

"But ever since Father lost all his money, we've lived on mutton," said Mick, contemplating the leg moodily.

"You're not to go on saying that, Mick." said Mrs. Felton. She turned to Tess with a worried frown. "He will keep saying it, and it makes it so sad for Father. It's not as if he lost it all, anyway, is it, Hugh?"

Mr. Felton, placidly slicing the meat, was quite unmoved. "Fortunately," he said, "we still have enough to keep a rag on the boys' backs until they're old enough to do a job of work. What more can we want?"

After dinner the two girls and Mick washed up while Dick took Jack off for a last-minute check of their gear. Mrs. Felton sent them all off to bed early, telling them not to be late for breakfast.

"As if we would," said Dick. "Tomorrow, of all days."

"I know, dear," said Mrs. Felton. "But breakfast's at half-past six. Murphy's coming at seven, you know."

"Well, you weren't supposed to get up, anyway," said Dick.

"Wasn't I?" said Mrs. Felton in surprise. "Well, I'm not missing the fun, so go along now and don't argue."

"Peace, brother," said Mick, giving Dick a push toward the door. "We'll give her breakfast in bed when we get back. I'll make her an omelette."

They said good night, and as they went off, Dick said to Tess, "He will, too, you know. He's a wizard in the kitchen—funny kid."

Pat and Tess slept dreamlessly and were waked the next morning by Jack's voice at the window. "You'd better beat it to the bathroom while you've got the chance. There's a bit of competition."

As she had promised, Mrs. Felton had breakfast ready

punctually at half-past six. And even at this hour she looked fresh and immaculate. She seemed, in fact, as excited as any of them. "Now sit down and eat as much as you can," she said. "Heaven knows when you'll eat again."

The dismal prophecy had a gratifying effect, and they all ate large quantities of porridge, eggs, and toast in the shortest possible time.

They were just adding the last articles to the now formidable pile by the back gate when Tess, hearing the faint throb of an automobile engine, looked up to see a vehicle moving along the track from the main gate. It was a car of the type once described as an open tourer, and open it certainly was, but one would have thought its touring days were done. The canvas top was moored only tenuously to the body, and every so often a gust caught it so that it filled out like a parachute. The whole effect was one of frailty, age, and eccentricity.

"Whoever's that?" said Tess in astonishment.

Mick and Dick looked up quickly. Their faces brightened, and they shouted together, "It's Murphy! Hey, Jack, are you ready? He's here."

"Who's Murphy, exactly?" asked Tess.

"He's the cove who's taking us to the foot of the mountains," said Dick. "He drops us there, and we meet the guide and the ponies."

Jack came hurrying from where their utility was parked, carrying the last roll of blankets and a gridiron, with Silver bounding around him in circles.

"That dog enters into the spirit of the thing," said Mick pensively.

Jack dropped the bundle on top of the others and stood

beside the other four watching the stately approach of their conveyance. "Geraldine's twin sister," he said after a pause.

"Elder sister, I think," said Pat.

By the time it reached them, a thin plume of steam was already issuing from the radiator cap. It stood vibrating violently for a moment. Then the driver turned off the engine and climbed out. He was not very tall, but in what Uncle John would have called prime condition. His clothes were greasy and had, in the course of time, acquired bulges and folds to suit his anatomy, and a uniform shade of plains' dust. He had the face of a brigand, but his eyes twinkled as he smiled at them.

"Well, are yous ready?" he asked in a throaty rumble.

"All ready, Murphy," said Dick. "Shall we fill her up?"

"I'll load her meself," he said cautiously. "You bring what's to go."

"It's all here," said Dick, pointing to the pile.

Murphy looked at it in silence. Then he took off his hat and scratched his head. After another few moments' thought he said, "And you five—and the dog?"

"That's right," said Dick.

Slowly Murphy's face broke into a smile. It widened until his eyes almost vanished in creases of pure enjoyment. "You're a caution," he said at last.

Then, with deliberation he attacked the pile. The boys fetched, carried, held, or tied as he ordered, and the girls watched in admiration. The back seat was piled without an inch to spare, one bundle was tied on the grid at the back, another on the front bumper and the running boards were loaded with boxes and bags strapped tight. A packsaddle was tied to the top, a hurricane lamp hooked on the radiator cap, and the car was ready.

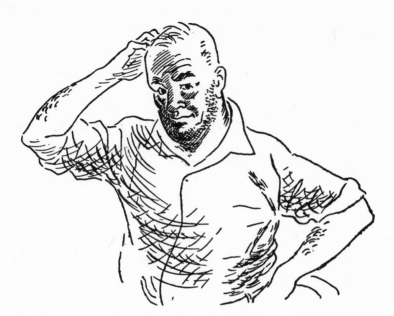

Murphy stood back and surveyed the job, adjusted a strap, and then dived in under the steering wheel, emerging with some difficulty holding half a dented kerosene tin.

"Can you get me a drop of water?" he asked. "I'll give her a drink before we start." He handed it to Mick, who looked at it for a moment as if it might have been an ancient Greek tear bottle, then, coming to life, took it and made for the house.

"I'll tell Mother," he shouted over his shoulder.

He returned with Mrs. Felton, who clasped hands in admiration when she saw the car.

"How *did* you do it, Murphy?" she asked.

"Done it before, Mrs. Felton," he said briefly.

"Well, I think you're wonderful," she said. "Now don't

go till Mr. Felton comes. He won't be a minute. And are you all quite ready now?" She turned to the others. "You girls have left your dresses here, have you? You won't want anything but your jeans till you come back. And I think you'd all better take coats. It'll be cold on the mountain, won't it, Murphy?"

Murphy nodded. "I rang Ted this morning to make sure he'd meet us with the ponies, and he reckoned there was a frost up there last night."

"There! You see?" said Mrs. Felton, gratified at such unimpeachable confirmation. "So be sure you're warm enough. What about woolen undershirts? Shall I run and get half a dozen of the boys' just in case?" She stood poised for flight, but Mick put a hand on her arm and looked solemnly into her face.

"We have them, Mother," he said earnestly.

As Murphy emptied the last drop of water into the car's steaming interior and screwed on the radiator cap, there was a step behind them, and Mr. Felton appeared. His eye traveled over the car, came to rest on Murphy's face, and a smile of understanding passed between them.

"Nice work, Murphy," he said. "I expect they've told you they want to stop at the baker and the butcher in Kullaroo, and then you can take them straight out. The sooner they reach the top, the better. They won't want to be putting up tents in the dark. I suppose Ted's quite reliable? We've rather left it in your hands."

Murphy nodded. "He was bred in the Karkoos, and he's a good, steady cove. They'll be right with him."

"Good," said Mr. Felton. "Time they learned to look after themselves, anyway. Good experience. Well, all aboard, everyone."

"Good-bye, dears," said Mrs. Felton, nodding, waving,

and smiling before they were even in the car. "Have a lovely time, and do be careful. They say there are some nasty precipices up there."

It took some thought and manipulation to fit themselves in, but they managed it at last—all but Silver, who balanced on a box on the running board with Jack's hand on his collar. Tess suggested that she should change places with him because, as she explained to Jack, her pedigree was not nearly so long, but he assured her that Silver was more used to running boards than she was. Murphy started up the engine, and they slowly turned and made off down the track to Kullaroo. Mr. and Mrs. Felton stood until the dust from their departure had settled and they were well away down the paddock. Then, for the first time, a shadow crossed Mrs. Felton's face.

"I suppose they'll all be perfectly safe?" she said.

"No one is ever perfectly safe anywhere," said Mr. Felton. "But unless they lose their little city friend, which is very unlikely, I can't see that they can get into any trouble at all."

She put her hand through his arm, and they walked slowly back to the house.

CHAPTER TEN

The
Climb

*T*hey did not stop long in Kullaroo. They bought their bread and their meat and set off again, turning north out of the town. In the distance ahead they could see the Karkoo Ranges, a dim blue mass on the skyline. There had been little rain here in the early spring, and the country through which they traveled was flat and bare and dusty. The dirt road lay yellow and uninteresting before them, without a bend or a twist. From time to time they passed small poverty-stricken homesteads, for the soil here, even in a good season, was poor. Occasionally in the treeless paddocks were groups of thin cattle. They did not see any sheep. There was nothing in the immediate prospect to enliven them, but Murphy, once settled comfortably behind his steering wheel and with the town behind him, started to talk. At first he made only odd remarks, brief announcements of the names of creeks or properties, but by degrees he warmed up and began a flow of reminiscence and anecdote that kept them enthralled as the miles fell away. As he talked he gesticulated with his hands, and their progress became erratic and exciting. They noticed also (it was Mick, directly behind him, who pointed it out to the others) that with the years the top of his hat had worn a hole in the lining of the canvas top. It seemed only a matter of time before he would be driving with an entirely unobstructed view, his head protruding through the top itself.

After a time they came to the end of the flat country. They were approaching the foothills, and the range ahead now looked larger, more solid, and infinitely higher. The shadeless plain gave way to timbered hills deep in grass and full of rocky outcrops. The road, as such, ended, and they passed onto a track through enclosed paddocks with many gates. As the old car wound its way deeper into the hills, bounding over boulders, concealed holes in the grass, and rocky creeks, it began to show its mettle. No well-bred car would have tackled such a track. The hills closed in around them, and the range ahead loomed every minute more rugged and menacing. For some time now they had seen no house nor any sign of life except an occasional rabbit.

At last, long after they thought the car must surely be forced to stop, they came to a little clearing by a creek. Here Murphy stopped. They got out, a little stiff after their cramped journey. Behind them wound the narrow valley through which they had come, and ahead the creek was swallowed up in the high hills and lost among tall gum trees and thick undergrowth. Tilting their heads backward, they could see, clear against the sky, the central peaks. One, massive and sharp, rose above all the others.

Murphy pointed. "See that?" he said. "That's where you'll be tonight. That's Calca."

If any of them, gazing upward, had any misgivings, they kept them to themselves.

It was Mick who spoke first. "Five thousand and two feet," he said. "And Kullaroo is seven hundred feet above sea level." He sat down suddenly, picked up one dusty boot, and laid it almost reverently on his other knee. "Will you do it, old friend?" he asked musingly. "Four thousand feet this afternoon? That's two thousand for you and two thousand for your mate here." He leaned forward and patted the other boot with thoughtful kindness. Then he jumped up. "Well," he said. "What are we waiting for?"

Pat, who did not know him as Dick and Jack did, looked at him in astonishment, but Tess gave a gurgle of laughter.

"He propitiates his gods," she said.

"Yous Feltons," said Murphy resignedly, pushing his hat back on his forehead. "Come on. You can help me unload the car. Ted'll be along any minute now."

The first moment of awed wonder passed. This was the real beginning of the expedition. They fell upon Murphy's old car like locusts, and very soon the ground around it was strewn with the necessities of open-air life.

"Hey!" said Murphy anxiously. "Give me room to back out."

"Back out?" said Dick. "What do you want to back out for? You can't go yet."

"Poor cove wants to get back to his dinner," said Jack, looking with pity at Murphy's well-filled belt.

"Well, he can't," said Dick. "He's having dinner with us. Brought a lot extra specially."

"Oh," said Murphy, brightening visibly. "That's different. Want me to start a fire?"

"What about Ted?" asked Dick. "He'll have to have some. Think we should wait?"

"Wait for Ted?" said Murphy. "Don't you. He'll be along. Anyway, he's a terrible good doer—goes for miles on a dry crust and a rag soaked in milk. We'll start." He bent laboriously to pick up one or two small sticks that lay at his feet, but Tess, who was hopping around in a high state of excitement with nothing for the moment to do, pushed him gently backward onto a nearby log.

"Sit down," she said. "And take that hat off. I'll light the fire. It's one of the things I've learned to do."

But even then she was forestalled. Pat, in her quiet and efficient way, had already begun the fire on the other side of the clearing, and the blue smoke was beginning to trickle upward. Tess went over to help her, and the boys, unable to keep still for long, strolled among the packages. "Making a final check," they called it, and Tess tactfully refrained from inquiring why it should be necessary at this stage. Once Mick stopped for several minutes and gazed, motionless, into the blue sky.

"What is it?" asked Jack. "Airplane?"

Mick shook his head, his eyes still in space. "Smell," he said. "Strange smell—like rotting corpses. Can't think what it's doing among the blankets."

Jack walked over and stood beside him. He sniffed. "You're right," he said. "That's odd." He bent down, hands on knees, and studied the packages at his feet. Suddenly he stiffened. "Oh," he said.

"Found it?" said Mick, bending down, too. "What is it? Dead cat or something?"

Jack straightened up. "Dead sheep, as a matter of fact," he said. "Silver's tucker."

Mick studied Jack's face with interest. "Mean to say you went to the trouble to bring a decomposing sheep for your dog?" he asked.

"Well," said Jack, slightly apologetic. "Not a whole sheep. Bones and things."

"And all well hung, packed up in your blankets," pursued Mick. "All among *our* blankets, too, if it comes to that."

Jack waited, a little guilty, for he had forgotten the "nice ripe bones," but the outburst he expected did not come. Instead, Mick continued to look at him with all the interest of a scientist in an impaled insect, and then strolled on, shaking his head like an old man. "Queer thing," was all he said.

Just then Pat called to them to say that the billy was boiling. They were about halfway through their dinner when she suddenly said, "Listen!"

From among the trees behind them came the stamp of horses' hoofs and the creak of leather.

"That'll be Ted," said Murphy.

Silver barked and raced to the edge of the clearing. Out of the trees came five smallish ponies, four of them wearing empty packs, the fifth ridden (in an ordinary saddle) by a slim, dark man with sharp eyes and a bird-like face. He was younger than they had expected.

"Good day, Ted," shouted Murphy. "Nearly missed your tucker. Leave the ponies there and come and have your dinner."

Ted nodded to him with a slight grin, slid off his pony, leaving the reins trailing, and came to the fire.

"Sit down," ordered Murphy, and Ted walked over

and sat down beside him. The ponies stood where they were left, heads drooping.

"Better meet your family," said Murphy. "Now let's see if I got it right." He looked at Tess, who sat on his other side. For a moment his forehead wrinkled. "Er—Bess, no; Tess, this one." His brow cleared. "Then Jack, Pat, Dick, and Mick." Ted nodded to them each in turn. He did not seem a man to waste words. They handed him a mug of tea and some sardines on bread and butter, and he began his dinner in silence.

Pat, who had been looking at the thin, sleepy ponies with some dismay, now turned to Ted. "Those ponies," she began, "are they—will they—we have rather a lot of stuff; do you think they're strong enough? It looks such a long way."

Ted nodded. "They're all right," he said briefly.

"Don't you worry about them," said Murphy with a broad smile. "They don't look much, but you wait till they start climbing."

As soon as they had finished, the boys jumped up. The sun was high overhead by now and blazing down into the clearing. Very soon the best of the day would be past, and the peak still lay ahead. They started to collect bundles, but Ted stopped them.

"Leave 'em," he said. "I'll pick 'em up from there."

"You let him do it," said Murphy, settling himself on a log. "He's done all this before, and you don't want them packs unrolling halfway up the mountain." He leaned comfortably on his elbow and prepared to watch, while Ted picked up one bundle after another and stowed it away on the ponies. To Jack, who was now in a fever to get started, he seemed to work with agonizing slowness. Dick, unable to contain himself, burst into song, and

Murphy, after a moment's stunned surprise, joined in, too. Tess, recognizing the tune, added her voice, and in a moment they were all "Rolling Down the Mountain" with a will. Silver sat down and howled.

"Hey!" said Murphy.

"It's only the top note he doesn't like," explained Jack.

"Too bad," said Murphy. "I'm a tenor myself, too."

But Ted was cording up the last pack. All four pack ponies now stood, almost invisible beneath their billowing white packs. All one could see of them was a head, a wispy tail, and four little sticks of legs.

"Are you *sure* they're strong enough?" asked Pat.

"Course they are," said Murphy scornfully. "Look at 'em. They don't even notice the packs is on them."

It was true; they did not appear to notice anything.

Ted brought them together and tied the halter of one to the tail of the one before. The first stood with its halter trailing, and only the saddle pony stood aloof. Around its saddle hung various articles that had been overlooked: a frying pan, a large tin spoon, a rolled mackintosh, and somebody's hairbrush.

"Mick's, of course," said Dick.

"So it is," said Mick. "Must have fallen out of my pocket. It'll be safer there."

"If sweaty," added Dick.

Ted turned to them. "You can take turns on the saddled one," he said. "And it'll be all right to ride on the pack ponies for a while." Ted grasped the halter of the first pony and swung himself onto the pack. Tess, Pat, and Mick climbed onto the other pack ponies, and Dick got onto the saddle pony. Jack said that he would keep Silver company in the rear. Murphy got to his feet.

"Well, cheerio," he said. "I'll be back in five days' time to pick up what's left of you." His desperado's face creased into a parting smile. Ted pulled his pony's head up, gave it a slap on the shoulder, and the cavalcade moved off with Silver capering around Jack behind them. They headed into the thick scrub ahead, and the last they saw of civilization was Murphy standing beside his car waving his hat.

After a short time they found themselves scrambling along the bed of a stony creek. There was only a small trickle of water in it, but the stones were jumbled together awkwardly and made the going difficult. They were surrounded now with tall trees that blotted out the sun, so that they rode in a damp, sweet-smelling gloom full of the sound of birds. On either side, enclosing them, rose the steep hillsides, and as they wound their way up the creek, the horses' sides were brushed by maidenhair fern and wildflowers.

"What does it feel like, being part of a pack?" shouted Dick.

"Fine," answered Tess. "Just like being a sultan on an elephant." She wriggled more securely into the white, enveloping folds.

"Speak for yourself," said Mick. "I think I'm sitting on the billy."

Presently, after they had climbed some distance they left the creek and took to the steep hillside. Tess, hearing a plop behind her, looked around. Mick had slid off his pony and had joined Jack at the rear. "Too many corners in my pack," he explained.

The track became steeper all the time, but now the trees were thinning out a little, and once or twice they caught glimpses of Calca high above them. It looked higher than ever, and they could clearly see its rugged sides. Pat and Tess began to feel that their packs were wearing thin, and balancing was difficult on the steep slopes. Pat called to Ted, and he stopped while they slid off. Dick offered them his pony, but they decided to walk, so Jack changed places with Dick. They proceeded again in silence. There was no breath left for talking, and there was something about these massive hills and shadowed gorges that discouraged conversation.

The ponies walked on, threading their way through saplings and around fallen trees, surefooted and steady. But it was not until they were about halfway up that they really proved themselves.

Rounding a bluff, they came face to face with a great barrier of rock. On either side the mountain fell away sharply. The rocky bottoms of the gorges were visible far below, and at the end of each, as it opened out in the distance, were the foothills through which they had traveled in Murphy's car. High up, over tumbled boulders, was a small gap in the rocks. Ted stopped the ponies and slid off.

"He'll never get the ponies through there," said Dick as a little breath came back to him. But Ted, without hesitating, led the ponies up the rocks. In spite of the packs they climbed like cats, choosing their steps carefully, slipping and sliding on the round stones but never losing balance. Where they couldn't climb, they jumped, each following the one before. When they came to the gap, they slid through, one after the other. The packs brushed the rock on either side.

"Cripes!" said Jack. He gave the pony its head and leaned forward. After him scrambled the others. Ted waited until they were all through and then started off again.

The sun was getting lower now, and Pat, tramping solidly along, looked above her. Calca still towered over them. It seemed a long way off. She glanced around at Tess, who trudged after her with puce cheeks and bent head. She lifted it as Pat turned, and grinned.

"Excelsior!" she gasped.

Gradually the slope became less steep, the undergrowth thinned out to almost nothing, and once or twice over a dark sea of hills they caught glimpses of the distant plains. But to all of them now each step became an effort. Even Silver trotted, panting, at Jack's heels. Tess, forcing herself onward, began to wonder if the climb would ever end.

So tired were they that they scarcely noticed when they ceased to climb and walked instead along level turf among tall straight trees.

They were all taken by surprise when Ted stopped the ponies and said, "We're here."

"Here?" said Dick in surprise. "Where's Calca?"

Ted pointed to the right of them. The peak they had been watching all day, the unapproachable, rugged summit, stood at their elbows only a few hundred yards away.

"Best put up the tent before it gets dark," said Ted, beginning methodically to unload the ponies.

"But what about Calca?" asked Pat, who liked to finish a job once started. Ted looked at her with a faint but approving grin. "Ain't you had enough yet?" he asked. "You can climb up in the morning before breakfast if you want. Too late now."

So Pat, with Tess's help, went off to start the fire for supper. The last pack slipped to the ground, and while the boys began unfolding the tent, Ted led off the ponies. Passing Tess, who was collecting sticks, he said, "Better bring the billy. I'll show you the water." Tess ran back to fetch it and caught up with him again as he waited for the ponies to drink at an unexpected trickle of water.

"Up there," he said, pointing to where the tiny stream ended among moss-covered boulders.

Following it up, Tess found that the rocks concealed a small, clear pool fringed with fern. Just above it the water bubbled out from among the stones.

"Oh," she said with delight. "It's a spring." She bent down to drink before she filled the billy. The water was ice-cold and fresh with a faintly mineral tang.

Ted turned the ponies into a small yard nearby, made of saplings lashed to the trunks of trees.

"Every convenience," said Tess.

"Can't have 'em going home on us," explained Ted.

When they got back to the camp, the fire was blazing, and the boys were hammering the pegs in around the tent. Under the tall trees and the vast sky it looked like a small home for them all for four nights.

Their camping place, they found when they had time to look around, was situated on a saddle between Calca and its adjacent peak. Now that the first blue shadows of night were flowing up through the tree trunks, they noticed that the air had a sharp nip very different from the heavier atmosphere of the plains. The trees and scrub, and even the grass up here, were the authentic growth of a colder climate. They still carried the tangy smell of growing things brought out by the warmth of the day. But Ted, glancing at the cloudless violet of the sky, said, "Frost tonight, shouldn't wonder."

The bush at this hour was very still. There was no wind. Once or twice a belated bird flew over, high and at speed, and once a magpie called from farther off in the brush. The boys finished the tent and came up to the fire. Tess was making toast, one arm shielding her face from the flames. Pat was slicing onions into the frying pan.

"What's to be done?" asked Dick.

"There's another billy somewhere," said Pat. "It has the butter in it."

"Right," said Dick obligingly, and began to hunt among the packages. They heard him give a satisfied grunt as he dragged a large billy from a roll of bedding. There was a pause, and then they all jumped as he exclaimed loudly, "Great blistering Jupiter! What's this?"

They looked around to find him with the lid in one hand, staring into the billy. Then he put in his hand gingerly and slowly brought it out, holding a battered, off-white object that seemed, in the flickering firelight, to regard them all with a remote and baleful eye. Tess gave it one glance and lost her balance as she burst into a peal of laughter.

"Oh, Christmas," said Jack.

Pat gave one high little gasp and then looked at Dick. "It's Pinkie," she said weakly.

"Who is Pinkie?" asked Dick in the patient voice one uses to small children and lunatics.

It was obvious that a development of this kind was new in Ted's camping experience, for he sat down suddenly on a log and regarded them all in apprehensive silence. Only Mick stood quietly, a light of intelligent interest in his eyes as he studied the eccentric contours of Billy's straying lamb. Now he answered Dick.

"That thing's Pinkie, you idiot," he said reasonably. "What I want to know is who brought it."

"He must have gotten into the billy by mistake," said Pat, feeling the explanation was hardly adequate.

Mick's dark eyes absorbed her steadily for a moment. "You Steadmans are a funny lot," he said. "Question is, where's the butter?"

But Jack had recovered and felt that family honor required an explanation. "Pinkie is my young brother's toy lamb," he said crisply. "Billy must have put him there when we weren't looking."

"He said Pinkie wanted to come," said Tess. "I remember now. And when we left, he did look as if he were bulging with a secret."

"And that funny noise he made at breakfast," added Pat.

"Well," said Jack. "Pinkie's here, and as Mick says, where's the butter?"

It was found, after a prolonged search, wrapped in Jack's spare shirt. For two days it had been well protected against the cold and was now approximately at the temperature of an incubated egg.

Preparations for supper continued. The smell of fried onions mingled with the night scents of the bush. The billy came to the boil with an angry hiss, and mugs were passed around. They did not sit long over their meal, for there was still unpacking to be done, and although supper revived them a little, they were still very tired.

Pat and Tess were to sleep in the tent, and the boys, scorning such soft treatment, went off to spread their sleeping bags on the lee side of the first log they found. Ted prepared to sleep by the fire, for he carried only one thin blanket and a groundsheet. One by one they went off to the spring, each with a towel and a toothbrush; one by one they said good night and wandered off into the darkness. Pat and Tess spread out their blankets in the tent and crawled into them. Through the open flap they could see the fire still leaping brightly, for Ted had stoked it up, and Ted himself was a dark and motionless mound beside it, his head on a saddle. Once Silver trotted up, put his head into the tent, and whined. They heard Jack whistle softly, and Silver bounded off.

"Night," said Tess, yawning.

"Sleep well," said Pat, and turned over in the darkness.

CHAPTER ELEVEN

Misty Mountaintops

*T*ess, who had never slept on the ground before, woke up once or twice in the night to change her position and rub her numbed hip. Each time, hearing Pat's deep, regular breathing, she experienced a sense of grievance that her faithful friend should be so inconsiderately asleep when she was awake. But when she woke for the last time, it was to find the first shadowless light of the day flowing into the tent. This time, as she rolled over, she saw Pat lying quietly beside her, her eyes wide open.

"Good morning," said Pat. "How do you feel?"

"Wonderful," said Tess sleepily, "except that I'm stiff, and my feet are freezing."

"So are mine," said Pat. "It was a cold night."

"I didn't think you noticed it," said Tess. "Every time I woke, you were sound asleep."

"And every time I woke, you were sound asleep," said Pat. They both laughed, and Pat wriggled around onto her elbow and lifted her head to look out of the tent.

"The grass is all white with frost," she said in astonishment. "No wonder we were cold. But the fire's still going, so I expect Ted's up."

"Then let's get up, too," said Tess, sitting up. "I really think I've had enough of my inner springs for one night."

They slipped their clothes on quickly, snatched their towels and toothbrushes, and raced for the spring. The water was colder than ever, but crystal clear and limpid in the early light. Ted and Silver were warming themselves by the fire when they reached it. There was no sign of the boys.

"Morning," said Ted. "Cold night."

They warmed their hands by the blaze for a few minutes, and then Pat started to get breakfast.

"Eggs and bacon this morning," she said. "You watch the boys crawl out when they smell the bacon."

She was quite right, for it was not long after the first few rashers had begun to sizzle in the pan that Jack and Dick appeared from the scrub. They looked tousled and sleepy, but their eyes lit up when they saw that preparations for breakfast were under way.

"Good work," said Dick approvingly. "I'll have a wash and be with you in a minute."

They were all thawing out into bland contentment and the sun was sending the first yellow shafts across the grass when Mick appeared.

"The butler had orders to bring me breakfast in bed," he said. "But when food doesn't come to me, I go to it— reasonable." He picked up an enamel plate and scooped a generous helping of eggs and bacon onto it from the frying pan.

"Everyone sleep well?" he asked. "Some darned great animal nearly put its foot on my face."

"Scrub cattle," said Ted. "Half a dozen of 'em came up to look at the fire."

"Did they?" said Tess in surprise. "I didn't hear a thing."

"I told you you slept well," said Pat.

"Where do you want to go this morning?" asked Ted when they had finished breakfast.

"Calca," they all said together. So when the camp had been tidied and the beds folded, Ted led them up the peak.

At first they walked up a steep, grassy slope that took the wind out of them very quickly. The trees and scrub stopped short of the peak itself, and they traveled over open ground. Even the grass at the end gave up the struggle, and they climbed the last few dozen feet up bare rock and loose stones. The top of Calca was several yards square, a giant's pile of rocks and stones.

They stood close together, braced against the cold wind. On every side they could see out over the dark blue sea of hills and gorges to the plains beyond. Here and there in the boundless expanse of flat country little hills popped up like mosquito bites. Already, down below, the day looked hot and dusty. But here the freshness of the morning still lingered, and the wind had the bite of high places.

"How far can we really see?" asked Jack.

"About a hundred miles on a clear day," answered Ted.

They picked out Kullaroo and the creek, a tiny thread in the distance, and Dick was explaining exactly where to find the Felton house when Mick interrupted.

"You coot," he said. "That's the Kullaroo railway siding. You know we can't see the peak from home."

Tess, turning around to look in the other direction,

exclaimed, "Oh, goodness, there's the sea! Whatever is it doing here?"

But Ted, his smile evident for once, said, "Looks like it, doesn't it? That's the Pilliga scrub."

"You mean just bushes and things?" said Tess in surprise.

"That's all," said Ted.

They stayed for a short time longer, for this moment, after all, was the reason for the whole expedition, and even if they were stiff with cold, it seemed a pity to cut it short. Down below, following Ted's pointing finger, they saw their track of the previous day, winding and twisting around the shoulders of the hills, plunging into gorges that the sun this morning had not yet reached. Between them and the tops of trees far below, a number of wedge-tailed eagles hovered motionless.

"What are they doing, just hanging there?" asked Tess.

"Waiting for their breakfast," said Ted. "They ain't as lucky as us."

By the time they reached camp again, it was time for lunch. They lingered over it, drowsing in the warm sun. No one seemed inclined to be energetic. Mick, lying on his back, gazed thoughtfully up to where Pinkie rested, for safety, in the crotch of a tree.

"Can't make it out," he said. "What's the strength of that animal, anyway? Must be more than a toy. You all take it so seriously."

Tess sat up. "That lamb is a horrid little beast," she said with unexpected heat. "It always knows best; it does everything better than anyone else, it makes me fall off the pony, and it's always popping up where it's least expected."

Jack gave a shout of laughter. "And when it's sick," he

added, "it always has the most horrible diseases. And Billy adores it. It's his ego."

"You see," said Pat to Mick. "We're all really rather fond of Pinkie."

"I don't see," said Mick. "Tess doesn't seem to care for it much."

"That was because Pinkie took advantage of her when she came to the country for the first time," said Pat seriously.

"There you are, you see," said Mick. "You talk as if the darned thing were real. I give up." Then a thought struck him, and he looked carefully at Tess. "Are you from the city, then?" he said at last. Tess nodded.

"A city girl?"

"Yes," said Tess.

"Lived all your life in town?"

"Yes," said Tess again.

"She can swim like a porpoise," said Pat defensively.

"Not much use here," said Mick reasonably. He continued to study Tess and then nodded his head twice, slowly. "We'll have to watch you," he said. "You'll be getting lost."

"Of course she won't," said Pat indignantly.

"Oh, yes, she will," said Mick. "They all do. Look at the tourists in the Blue Mountains. Get lost in shoals every day. Sure to."

"Not if I can help it," said Ted quietly.

The afternoon was wearing on when Dick at last jumped to his feet and said, "I'm going up the peak on the other side of this saddle before it gets too late. Anyone coming?"

"I'll come," said Jack. He turned to Ted. "Is it OK?" he asked.

Ted nodded. "You can't miss it," he said. "But don't go any farther, or you'll end up going over one of the cliffs in the dark."

"Right," said Jack, and he and Dick went off through the trees followed by Silver. For a time the others could hear the crash of trampled undergrowth and broken twigs and the sound of voices, but presently the crashing became fainter, the voices reached them only spasmodically, and at last the noise died away altogether. The small sounds of the bush became audible again: a bird, high up in the branches overhead, the rustle of swinging bark, two branches squeaking, a frog down by the spring.

The light was beginning to fade when Tess yawned, got up, and said, "I think I'd like to sleep right outside tonight. I'm going to find a nice soft place and spread my blankets before it gets dark. You don't mind, Pat?"

"I will, too, then," said Pat, following her. "I couldn't see the moon last night."

By the time they had returned and built up the fire for supper, it was almost dark. There was still no sign of the boys. Ted said, "Reckon I'd better go and give them a coo-ee." He went off with Mick while Pat and Tess put on the billy, laid out an impressive row of chops on the gridiron, and started to make the toast. In the distance they could hear Ted coo-eeing, a high, lost sound that echoed among the hills.

"You can't tell whether it's an echo or a reply," said Tess.

"No," said Pat. "But I'm sure they're all right. Jack would never get lost."

Tess suddenly put down the loaf and the knife and turned to Pat, her face glowing and sparkling in the firelight. "Oh," she said, "isn't it wonderful here? I shall never forget this."

"I'm so glad," said Pat with pleasure. "It's been much more fun with you here, too."

The chops were exploding and crackling in the fire when they heard the voices of the others. Pat looked around. Four dark figures loomed up. She counted them quickly.

"Oh, good," she said with a touch of relief in her voice. "You found them all right, then?"

"Found them?" said Mick in disgust. "They weren't even lost. Just sitting there looking at the view and talking about spark plugs."

"Spark plugs my foot," said Dick. "Crawler tractors, if you must know." He sat down and pushed his feet toward the fire. "Frostbitten, I think," he said in explanation.

After supper they settled themselves comfortably around the fire and talked.

Jack said to Ted, "Do you always have to be so careful about people getting lost? I mean, do you often lose 'em?"

"I never lost anyone yet," said Ted with a grin. "But you can get lost here easy. In the dark it's dangerous—them cliffs."

"Anyone ever been lost for good?" asked Dick.

"Can't recall anyone in my time," said Ted slowly. "They say there was a stockman once—" He paused. "There's a valley down there in the scrub. Some say you hear 'im of a night riding up and down, crackin' 'is whip, and callin' 'is dog."

"Is he—is he *real*?" asked Tess in a whisper.

"Should say not," replied Ted. "Happened about fifty

year ago." There was a pause. In the silence the fire flickered and popped. Ted grinned again. "I never seen 'im," he said.

"They say a dog always knows," said Tess.

They all turned their heads, though the boys denied it afterward, to look at Silver. He lay beside Jack, his nose between his paws, his eyes closed.

"Ghosts are for kids," said Dick firmly. "But lots of things happen that are just as funny as ghosts. Look at the *Marie Celeste*."

"Who was she?" asked Pat. And Dick told them the story of the ship found deserted in mid-ocean—the classic story that has never been explained. They talked of the Abominable Snowman, whose footsteps were seen by so many climbers on the slopes of Everest but who seemed himself to be invisible. One by one they remembered odd stories told by travelers and seamen, stories that had no end and that could not be explained. Around them the bush darkened, the stars came out above the treetops, and the leaves rustled gently in the night breeze.

Suddenly, above their heads, there came a scratching and a quick slither, and a dark object hurtled down, landing with a plop in the ashes. Tess, Ted, and Dick jumped to their feet. The other three threw up their legs hurriedly and crouched ready to move. It was Ted who stepped to the fire, bent down, and picked up the object. He held it up in the firelight.

"Oh," said Tess. "We might have known."

"See what I mean?" said Mick.

It was Pinkie.

"But why did he fall?" said Pat.

"I reckon a possum got a bit too inquisitive," said Ted. "That noise sounded like a possum."

"I wonder if he decided what Pinkie was before he fell," said Dick. "That possum might spend the rest of his life wondering now."

"Just another unexplained story," said Tess.

But Pinkie's descent had broken the spell. The other three got up, and one by one they made for bed. Tess crawled into her blankets and settled herself in the deep grass beside a log. She gave a long sigh of contentment as she looked up at the branches overhead and the bright stars above them. The moon had not yet risen, but farther off on the edge of the glade a group of trees shone milkily in its first rays. The frog still croaked by the spring, but that was the only sound there was. Her eyes closed.

It seemed only a few minutes later that they flew open again. Her heart was pumping fast, and still half-asleep, she quickly raised herself on her elbow and twisted her head to look behind her. She knew, though she could not remember how, that something had touched her hair. There came a gusty breath and a crash behind her, and she was just in time to see a startled kangaroo bound off around the end of the log. She smiled, her heart resumed its normal rhythm, and she settled down again. The moon, which those few moments before had not yet climbed above the horizon, now floated clear of the trees directly above her. The glade was flooded with its lemon-white light. The kangaroo must have visited Ted as well, for a crash from the direction of the fire and a shower of sparks indicated that he was awake and stoking up again. The air on her face was sharp and cold, and the blanket under her chin felt wet with dew. She withdrew like a tortoise into its shell and knew no more until a voice said, "Are you ever getting up this morning?"

She opened one eye and found herself looking into Pat's bright face. It took her some time to struggle from the depths of sleep, but presently she moved her head and brought the other eye into focus.

"Breakfast's ready," said Pat. This time her reaction was quicker. She sat up. The bush had resumed its normal daylight appearance. The moon had disappeared like a dream, and the grass and leaves sparkled in the warm yellow sunlight.

"I must have overslept," she said, blinking at Pat. "Shan't be a minute."

When breakfast was over, Ted took them in the opposite direction from Calca's peak. After walking through dense bush for some time, they came out on a flat strip of grassland that edged the bush and more or less encircled the peak that Dick and Jack had climbed the afternoon before. In front of them it fell away in sheer cliffs to the gorges and hills of the Karkoo Ranges far below.

"No wonder you thought we might go over here in the dark," said Dick, peering over. "It would be the easiest thing in the world."

Jack picked up a large stone and hurled it into space. They waited for a long time before they heard its muffled crash.

"I'm glad that wasn't me," said Tess.

"If it was you," said Mick, "it would be a sort of squelch." He looked upward. "You want to be like those fellows in a place like this."

They noticed then that there were many more wedge-tailed eagles on this side of the peak. The birds hovered only a little distance above their heads, eddying and gliding in the wind, and when later they stopped for a rest and lay on their backs in the grass, the eagles came to inspect them, floating on their huge wings so close above that they could see the feathered heads turn inquisitively this way and that, and the fierce claws tucked neatly underneath among the soft down.

The sun was high overhead by the time they reached the end of the long plateau. Just before they turned toward the scrub again, Pat said, "I can see some smoke down there. Not a bush fire so early in the season, surely?"

Ted looked carefully at the thin gray column rising out of the trees below. "I reckon that'll be a bunch of rabbiters," he said at last. "I heard they was coming up this way."

"They wouldn't make much out of the rabbits here, would they?" asked Jack. "I haven't seen many about."

"There's a fair few down there," said Ted. "But there's a rabbit-proof fence running away down in the gorge that stops 'em. They do quite well with traps along the fence."

Sometime late that afternoon when they were beginning to think of supper, Pat said to Jack, "What's happened to Silver? I haven't seen him for ages."

"He's about somewhere," said Jack. "He was with us this morning."

"I don't believe that I've seen him since we were on the plateau," said Tess.

"The old devil's probably found a dead sheep or something," said Jack comfortably. "He'll be along."

But there was no sign of Silver when they turned in that night. Jack still refused to be worried, saying that he knew how to look after himself and he'd turn up before morning.

During the night the wind rose, and when they woke the next morning, it was blowing strongly from the west, the branches above their heads whipping and thrashing like a rough surf. There was still no sign of Silver. Jack, at last, began to think that something must be wrong.

"I'll just walk around the plateau again," he said when breakfast was over. "If he's anywhere about, he'll hear me whistle."

"Not in this wind," said Dick.

But Ted would not let him go alone, and in the end they all went. They walked the whole length of the plateau, leaning against the wind that roared up from the valleys below. They could no longer see the plains beyond the range, for the air was full of dust. There was no sign of the rabbiters of yesterday.

Jack whistled and called, but the sound was whipped away as soon as it was uttered, and they knew that Silver would not hear. Sometimes they stopped to listen for a bark or a howl, but they soon realized that that was hopeless, too. The wind drowned everything.

They returned to the camp, hoping he would be there to greet them. But he was not, and Jack was sure now that something had happened to his dog. The question was, what? There were so many things that might have happened, but so few of them were at all likely.

"He could be stuck in a log somewhere, going after a rabbit," said Dick.

"Except that we haven't seen any rabbits," said Jack gloomily. "And he knows he's not supposed to chase them, anyway."

"Got his collar caught on a stake, maybe," suggested Ted.

"Doesn't wear one," said Jack.

"Could he possibly have fallen over the cliff?" asked Tess.

Jack shook his head. "Even a stupid dog wouldn't be likely to do that. I'd bet my last shilling Silver wouldn't go over unless he was pushed."

"Well, there's nothing to push him up here," said Mick. "Unless those eagles—" Suddenly he stopped. Then he turned to Ted. "Where did you say those traps were set?" he asked.

"Way down in the gorge there," said Ted. "And I don't even know that these coves are using traps."

"He'd never have gone all the way down there, surely?" said Pat.

"Don't see how he could," answered Ted. "There's no way down the cliffs, even for a dog. He'd have to go way back the other way and round the foot of the plateau. He'd never do that."

"Could he have been bitten by a snake?" asked Pat.

"Not this weather," said Ted firmly.

There seemed no answer and nothing to do for the moment but get themselves something to eat.

Lunch was an uneasy meal. Sparks kept blowing on them from fire no matter which side they went; leaves and dirt blew into the tea; pieces of paper and towels or jackets once hung up on convenient branches littered the clearing until Tess remarked that it looked like Bondi Beach on a Sunday afternoon; and over it all persisted the feeling of tension and anxiety. Every so often one of them would turn his head quickly to peer into the swirling scrub behind, thinking he heard something, but each time the wind, which can make any sound the ear expects, gave them the lie. There was very little conversation, for none of them felt that Silver's loss could be taken lightly. Both the Feltons and Ted knew that to lose a good sheep dog was a serious thing, and Pat and Tess felt that Jack could never be persuaded to leave the mountains until he knew what had become of Silver. It was taken as a matter of course that after lunch the search would start again. Murphy would be at the foot of the range to meet them the following day, and there was no time to spare.

So as soon as the meal was over, they packed up, threw everything that could not withstand the wind into the tent, and then knocked the pegs in more firmly with the ax. By common consent Ted now took charge of the search. He split them up, sending the boys to patrol one side of the peak, while he and the girls took the other. Each of them had a special landmark to aim at, and all were to return as soon as they had reached it. If that search failed, Ted would make for where he imagined the trapline of the rabbiters to be the following morning. It would delay their start until lunchtime, but it could not be helped. It was a last hope.

As he was directing them, Ted said, "It's bad enough losing the dog. I can't have you all lost as well. I dunno if I should let you go at all."

But they promised to do exactly as he said and to go no farther than the mark prescribed. When he came to Tess, he paused and frowned.

"You're from the city, ain't you?" he asked.

Tess nodded. "Yes. But please let me go. I'm not quite as silly as I look."

"I'm sure she'll be all right," said Pat, knowing what it would mean to Tess to be left to guard the camp.

"What about you two going together?" he said doubt-fully.

"Oh, please, no," said Tess. "That would be a waste of manpower, and *really* I'll be all right. I promise to be terribly careful. I quite realize that it would make hunting for Silver much more difficult if I got lost, too. And I do so want him to be found."

For a moment Jack's worried face softened. "I think she'll be safe enough," he said to Ted. "She's got her head screwed on, and she doesn't panic." He stepped across to the big tree near the fire, reached up, and took Pinkie from his perch in the branches. "Here," he said to Tess. "He mightn't be a particular friend of yours, but take him for company." He smiled for the first time since they had returned to camp as he tossed Pinkie over to Tess.

Tess caught him and tucked him under her arm. "If Pinkie can't find Silver," she said, "no one can."

Ted grinned briefly. "OK," he said. "But watch your step, and if you do get lost, sit down and wait. Don't go roamin' about." And he described her route very carefully.

At last he looked them all over, like a general reviewing his troops, and said, "I reckon we'll all be back here in about an hour and a half. If we ain't found him, I'll take a couple of you off again and we'll go farther down the slope—if there's any light left. But this'll do to begin with."

"Right, Ted," said Jack. "Thanks."

They went off, each to his own point in the circumference of a wide circle centering on their campfire. As they parted and disappeared, one by one into the scrub, their entity as a group was lost; each became one very small unit alone with the mountains and the bending trees and the shrieking westerly gale.

CHAPTER TWELVE

An Experience for Tess

*T*ess's path led past the spring and the ponies' yard and out in an easterly direction to where the saddle between the two high peaks sloped more gently to the source of a small creek. She was to walk on until she came to a clump of reeds that marked the creek, always facing a high cone of rock that rose like a medieval fortress on the far side of a deep abyss some way beyond the creek. Ted had told them once that the cone of rock, which had looked to them about the size and shape of a top hat, was in reality an acre in area. At the time it had seemed hard to believe, but now as she came nearer, she could see that it was a great bastion with steep sides towering into the sky. On her return she was to keep it directly behind her.

She walked quickly, but stopped to inspect every fallen log that she passed, remembering that Silver might have gotten jammed if he were after a rabbit. Every so often, too, she stopped to listen, but all she could hear was the swish and thrash of leaves, the groan of branch against branch, and the whine and whistle of the wind against her ears. Just occasionally she caught, somewhere in the distance, the sound of a tree falling—a long rending and tearing ending in a crash that seemed to silence for the moment all other sounds around it. And she began to look anxiously at the tortured trees above her, wondering which way she would jump if one of these became uprooted.

Now, for the first time, she began to feel very much alone. The bush was no longer friendly; it was fighting its own battles, and there were forces loose among the mountains that reduced a mere human to insignificance; among which, in fact, a human had no place at all. She found herself clutching Pinkie, finding in him her one link with a familiar, safe world. For a moment, overwhelmed by the violence about her, she forgot why she was here at all. Then she remembered Silver again, the sense of desolation left her, and recalling that damp, friendly nose in the palm of her hand on the Talia railway station, she stepped out more firmly, ashamed that she could have forgotten him for a moment.

She could see now, a little way beyond, a dark circle of green at the head of a rocky slope. This would be the clump of reeds that was her goal. Lower down the slope the trees grew more thickly again, and just above them a dark line that she took to be a fence snaked its way over a distant hill and disappeared. She had almost reached the reeds, which she could now see were a healthy group of bulrushes, when there came an ununexpected lull in the gale. For a moment, in contrast with the tumult that preceded it, was a silence so deep and sudden that it sang in her ears. Automatically she stopped to listen, and as she did so, from the very center of the brief silence, the long, low howl of a dog reached her. There was no mistaking it. She turned her head sharply, straining to catch it more surely. But now, with a burst of fury, as if its strength had been dammed up for that moment, the wind began again, and her chance was lost. She waited a little longer, but realizing it was hopeless, looked again in the direction from which she guessed the sound had come. Nothing alive moved at all on the rocky slope, and there was no sign of anything black and white among the grayish-green of lichened rock and grass. But farther down still was the dark belt of trees and, emerging from them, the long line of the fence. She looked about carefully, marking her bearings; then she took a deep breath and started to run down the slope.

When Pat returned to the camp, she found Mick sitting disconsolately beside the fire. He had thrown sticks on the smoldering logs and put the billy on. He raised a mournful eyebrow and shrugged his shoulders as she sat down beside him.

"Not a darned thing," he said. "No dog, not even the tiniest puppy. Rotten luck."

"Nor me," said Pat. "Never mind. One of the others may have found him."

But the others, as they came up one after another, told the same story. None of them had seen or heard anything.

Pat made the tea and handed around the mugs. Ted and Tess were still missing. They drank in silence as they waited. Presently there was a movement behind them and Ted appeared. Jack looked up quickly, but he shook his head.

"Been down among the cliffs," said Ted. "Couldn't see nothing there." He looked them over carefully and then said, "Where's the other girl?"

"Not come yet," said Pat. "But I'm sure she'll be along."

"She should be back," said Ted. "She had the shortest way of all."

Dick put down his mug carefully. "Might as well give her a chance to turn up," he said. "No sense in rushing off yet."

They waited. The sun was lower now. Another hour and a half would see the end of it. Pat filled up their mugs again, and they drank, glad of something to do. At the end of half an hour Ted got up. Jack sprang up after him, but Ted shook his head. "I'm going to see where she's got to," he said. "You'd all best stay here till I get back. We can't take no chances." Jack sat down again slowly.

After Ted disappeared, the time of waiting stretched out endlessly. Little by little the sun sank lower and the daylight began to fade. Pat, to give them all something to do, announced that she would direct the getting of the supper. As they worked, Dick and Mick made an effort at conversation, but Jack, absentmindedly slicing bread, said nothing, but glanced every few minutes at the setting sun.

He had thought—they had all thought—that losing Silver, who had thrown himself so wholeheartedly into the expedition, was as miserable a misfortune as could have befallen them. Now they realized they were on the brink of real tragedy. Meeting Murphy was no longer important; nothing was important any more except to find Tess. And here they sat, as the night came on, while Tess was—where? They dared not move until Ted returned, but each of them thought of the darkening cliffs, their jagged rims obscured by the thrashing grasses and the deceptive light.

Pat's voice suddenly broke the silence. "But she wasn't supposed to go anywhere near the cliffs."

"Easy enough to lose your sense of direction," said Dick. "Especially when—" He stopped abruptly.

"Especially if you're from the city," Jack finished for him savagely. "Why don't you say it? Everyone's been telling us she'd get lost. Well, now she has. How nice for them. And I sent her off. Ted didn't want her to go. But I sent her off to look for my dog." He jumped to his feet. "I'm going to find her."

"No, Jack," sad Pat sharply.

Dick got up quickly and caught his arm as he turned from the fire. "Don't be a fool," he said. "Nobody's blaming you. I know how you feel, but you'll only make things worse by charging off into the bush now."

Mick had not moved, but his eyes had not left Jack. Now he spoke quietly. "I don't believe she is lost."

For a moment Jack stood quite still; then he turned slowly. "How do you know?" he asked.

"Use your brains," said Mick. "She hadn't far to go; it was an easy route; and she went in broad daylight. Also, she may be strange to this sort of thing, but she's no fool. She may have twisted her ankle or been hit by a falling branch, or even, perhaps, found Silver. But I can't see how she could get lost."

Pat got up and put her hand on Jack's arm. "I agree with Mick," she said. "I've never thought she'd be silly enough to get lost, and I don't think so now. If people hadn't kept telling us that's what would happen to her, we wouldn't have been so sure it had. It's much more likely that she's"—Pat stopped suddenly, a catch in her breath—"that she's—hurt herself."

Nobody said anything for a moment, realizing that this solution, though more reasonable, made things no better than they were before.

By now the last of the daylight was draining away to the west. All color had disappeared from the bush, and only the fire, fanned by sharp gusts, glowed red and from time to time sent showers of firefly sparks into the dusk. For the time being there seemed nothing more they could say or do. Even Mick was standing up now beside the others, and four pairs of eyes peered, stretched wide to pierce the gloom, along the shadowed track that Tess had taken in sunshine those many hours before.

It seemed to each of them that they had been standing there for eternities of time when Pat's head went up quickly and she said, "Listen!"

For a few seconds they did not even breathe. Then, through the rustling and creaking overhead, they heard a faint coo-ee.

"Ted!" shouted Jack, and all four of them raced toward the sound.

A dark figure stepped from among the trees. After a moment they recognized Ted. He was bent down, holding something between his hands. They ran up to him, and he straightened up.

"Here you are," he said to Jack, pointing to his feet. "Got two of 'em anyway, and I reckon I know where the third is."

"Silver!" whispered Pat happily. And Silver, dusty, bedraggled, and weary, whimpered his joy and limped the last few steps to Jack. The sounds he made were

strangely muffled, for in his mouth was Pinkie. As Jack
reached out to pick him up, Silver thrust Pinkie into the
outstretched hands.

"Well, I'm darned," said Mick.

"Take him careful now," warned Ted. "His foot's
terrible sore. I don't know it isn't broken. He's been in
a trap."

Jack handed Pinkie to Pat and took his dog. Silver,
relieved of his burden, was giving little yelps half of
delight and half of pain, and his tail, under Jack's elbow,
waved indomitably.

"Met him coming out of the scrub just there," said
Ted, pointing. "I was on my way back when I saw him
with the lamb in his mouth. He was coming terrible
slow, but he wouldn't let me take it. Thought I'd better

let you know he was here before I went back for your friend."

"You know where she is?" asked Pat.

"I reckon I do, now that I see the dog," said Ted. "She'll be caught in a trap down on the fence there, letting him out. I mightn't of guessed except for seeing the lamb in his mouth." He nodded toward Silver. "You take him back to the camp. He's worth looking after, that dog." He turned quickly, and before they quite knew what he intended, he was racing back the way he had come. Jack handed Silver over to Pat, and with a brief, "Look after him," he made off after Ted, and this time he refused to be stopped.

By the time he and Ted reached the bulrushes only the faintest light remained in the open spaces. Under the trees it was quite dark. There was a keen bite now in the wind, and the wilderness about them was very desolate. Ted turned down the slope toward the trees.

"This way," he said, and hurried on without waiting for Jack.

But they never reached the trees. As they drew near, a dim, small figure came slowly toward them out of the shadows.

"Tess!" shouted Jack.

"Hello," answered Tess's voice, scarcely audible against the wind. They saw then that she carried her hands awkwardly in front of her.

"Hey!" said Ted. "Wait a minute," and bounded forward.

When Jack reached them, they were both crouched down. Then Ted made a quick movement with his foot, and they stood up. Ted supported Tess with one hand and in the other he held a rabbit trap.

"I'm such a fool," said Tess. "I've only just discovered you can pull these things out of the ground. I would have been back ages ago."

"She had it caught on her fingers," said Ted. He picked up her hand and felt the fingers with great care. Tess winced a little, but said nothing.

"Don't think they're broke," he said after a moment. "But they'll be pretty sore."

Jack, seeing the weariness in her face, stepped forward impulsively and put an arm around her shoulders.

"You found my dog," he said quietly.

For a moment the weariness vanished, and the old bright smile appeared on her face. "Did he come back?" she asked eagerly. "Did he? Oh, I'm so glad."

"He came back," said Jack.

"And now we're getting you back," said Ted. "Come on." He turned and flung the trap down the hill toward the fence. "Let 'em look for it," he said.

"Think you can make it to the camp?" asked Jack.

"Me?" said Tess in surprise. "Of course. I don't walk on my hands." And she started briskly up the hill to prove it.

Ted and Jack walked on either side of her. She insisted that she was able to walk by herself, but when after a short time they each took hold of her arm, she did not protest. She started to tell them what had happened, the reaction making her suddenly talkative, but Ted kindly but firmly told her she'd need her breath for the walk home. Once or twice a sudden twinge in the injured hand made her gasp, and then Ted would stop and massage the hand gently to restore the circulation. She made no complaint, but gradually their pace got slower, and it was a long time before they saw the gleam of the firelight between the trees.

"Journey's end," said Jack.

Tess had been silent for half an hour or more, but now she lifted her head and laughed softly. "I never thought that little tent would look so like home," she said.

"Wait till you've had a cupper tea," said Ted. "You won't know yourself." He whistled. There came an answering whistle, and three figures sprang up from around the fire and came crashing toward them.

"Oh, Tess," said Pat. "How glad I am to see you!" And she would have flung her arms around Tess, but Ted barred the way.

"Steady now," he said. "Her hand's pretty sore."

All five of them led her back to the camp. Everyone felt lightheaded with relief, and it became something of a triumphal procession. They made a great deal of noise, all talking at once and crashing happily through the scrub. Only the heroine herself, usually more alert than any of them, remained silent and stumbled a little as she walked.

When they reached the fire, Pat quickly made some tea, Mick produced a blanket and a pillow, and they would have sat her down there and then. But Tess stood looking about her a little vaguely. Then she saw Silver lying on a pile of sacks in the firelight. She stepped over to him, sat down, and put her good hand on his head. The black ears flattened, the shaggy tail waved gently, and he licked her nose.

"Dear Silver," she said softly.

CHAPTER THIRTEEN

Down to
the Plains
Again

Later, when she had disposed of several cups of
tea and a quantity of buttered toast and was sitting comfortably among her blankets and pillows, her hand
bathed and bandaged by Pat, she told them what had
happened.

"I'm afraid I wasn't very clever about it at all," she
began. "When I heard him howl, the sensible thing
would have been to rush back and tell you. But I was
too excited. I knew Ted would be cross with me"—she
smiled at Ted, who looked anything but cross as he
leaned against a log and surveyed his reassembled
charges—"but I *had* to run and have a look. I was
awfully careful about how to get back, and I wouldn't
have lost my way at all, but I didn't reckon on getting
caught like any silly rabbit."

"Might have happened to anyone," said Mick sooth-
ingly but untruthfully.

"I shouldn't think it would have happened to anyone
but me," said Tess. "Anyway, I rushed down to the trees

and walked along the fence. I had a bit of trouble discovering Silver because the silly dog stopped howling as soon as he heard me coming. That's the only silly thing I've ever known him do, as a matter of fact."

"They all do that," said Jack. "I suppose they think you're finding them by smell."

"Well, I wasn't," said Tess. "And it made it difficult, but I found him in the end. There he was, looking so tired and dirty with his poor paw caught in the trap right against the fence. The earth was scratched and dug up all around it where he had been struggling to get away, and the trap had teeth marks on it."

"Poor old Silver," said Pat, and, hearing his name, Silver lifted his head from the sacks and beat the ground with his tail.

"I didn't know how to get him out," went on Tess. "I tried all sorts of ways because, of course, I'd never seen a rabbit trap before. He was so pleased and excited that he kept trying to jump about, and I thought it would be the end of that poor mangled paw."

"You were lucky he didn't bite you," said Dick. "They often do when they're caught in a trap."

"Do they?" said Tess in surprise. "All Silver did was to lick my hand. At last I discovered I could move it by putting my foot on that spring thing, but I wasn't heavy enough to open it right up with my foot. So I had to pull with my hands, too. I got it open, and I was so pleased to see Silver's paw come out that I forgot all about my hands, and the next thing I knew, there I was —caught. All I could think about at first was how much it hurt and that Silver had had it like that for a whole day and a night. Then when I tried to undo it, I found I couldn't, and I began to think I'd be there for a day and a night, too. I—" Tess faltered suddenly. "I didn't care for that very much."

"I'll bet you didn't," said Ted. "Those traps hold on pretty tight."

"*Don't* they!" said Tess with deep feeling. "I didn't discover till just before Ted and Jack turned up that I could pull the stake out of the ground. It would have been easy if I'd realized. But when I seemed to be properly caught, I began to wonder how on earth I could let you know. There's not much you can do with only one hand when you start to try. Then I noticed that Silver had started to limp off up the hill. I thought it was a bit mean of him to leave me at first. And then I suddenly remembered Pinkie, and I thought that if I threw him, Silver just might take him home to Jack. I couldn't think of anything else to do, so I picked up Pinkie and threw him as hard as I could and called to Silver to take him home. Silver stopped and looked a bit puzzled. Then he noticed Pinkie just in front of him and went over to have a sniff. I thought he wasn't going to take him for a minute because he sat down to lick his paw. Then, when I almost thought it was hopeless, he scrambled up again, and I saw him pick Pinkie up. I could have screamed with excitement." She drew a deep breath. "Well, that's all, really. After that I just sat down and waited."

"Nothing to it," said Mick. "Just provide yourself with a dog like Silver and a toy lamb, and you've got it made."

"If it hadn't been for Pinkie," said Pat, "we might never have known you'd seen Silver at all. We would have thought the rabbiters had let him go."

"Wasn't it lucky?" said Tess. "And terribly clever of Silver, of course. But I never thought I should live to be so grateful to Pinkie. I shall start believing Billy now when he tells me all the things Pinkie does."

"Heaven forbid," said Jack. "But what I want to know is what were the traps doing along that fence. You didn't know they were there, did you, Ted?"

Ted shook his head. "Never guessed it. I thought they was trapping down there where we saw their fire. That's where I heard they'd be. Must have changed their camp yesterday, silly coots. They won't get much up this way."

"Well, we won't be losing any sleep over that," said Dick cheerfully. "And talking of sleep, isn't it time we put the invalids to bed?"

"It is," said Pat, jumping up. "But first I'm going to give you all a cup of cocoa, and I'm going to look at the wounds again."

So they sat peaceably sipping cocoa while Pat bathed Tess's hand and Jack attended to Silver. Tess's fingers were stiff and badly bruised, but the skin was not broken. Silver, who had struggled hard for much longer, was not so lucky. His paw was raw, and now that the circulation was returning, it was beginning to bleed. But Jack said he did not think it was broken. After a while he left Silver to lick it himself and came to sit down with the others.

The wind was dropping now as the night deepened, the fire died down, and peace fell on the little circle. After the increasing anxiety of the day and the tumultuous onslaught of the wind, the energy had run out of them all. They sat relaxed and happy, too tired to talk, too tired to go to bed. Tomorrow all this, the peaks and the high places, would be behind them. But although for a time they had feared otherwise, it would have a happy ending. After a while they got up, one by one, stretched, yawned, said good night, and drifted off.

As Tess climbed to her feet, she said apologetically, "I'm sorry I've caused so much trouble. I thought I was learning, too. But I'm just a mug from the city after all."

Mick, in the act of pulling on his sweater, stopped and looked at her. Then he said with deliberation, "You poor benighted imbecile, don't you realize you were the one who found the dog?"

Several times in the night Tess woke to feel her hand throbbing painfully and thought with sympathy of Silver. But in the morning, although her fingers were very swollen and now showed large purple bruises, the pain was better, and it was a happy cavalcade that set off down the mountain. The two invalids rode, Tess on the saddle pony with her hand in an improvised sling made out of her cardigan, and Silver securely wedged into one of the packs and looking faintly astonished.

The clearing, with its dead fire and trampled grass, looked forlorn and deserted behind them, but Calca on their left still pierced the sky, aloof and solitary in the morning sun. One wedge-tailed eagle, like a sentinel, hovered above it.

They had gone perhaps a quarter of a mile when Pat stopped in her tracks and said, "Oh, bother!" in a loud voice.

"Don't tell me," said Mick, who nearly bumped into her. "Let me guess." A wide smile spread across his face. "We've left Pinkie behind."

Pat nodded dolefully. Dick, behind them both, burst into a shout of laughter. "That lamb!" he said. "It's been a pleasure knowing it, and I shall go back and fetch it. Carry on. I'll be back in a minute." He went back up the track in long strides and caught up with them after a time with Pinkie under his arm. After four nights in the bush Pinkie had a travel-stained and experienced air, and one ear had been torn by the possum.

As they lost height, they could feel the warm, soft air of the plains gradually enveloping them, and it seemed no time before they were clattering and scrambling over the creek bed that opened out into the little clearing where Murphy was waiting for them.

He greeted them with fatherly enthusiasm, but shook his head over the two casualties. "That's bad," he said. "That's bad. What did you want to go and do a thing like that for?"

Tess, her eyes sparkling, said, "Experience."

When their gear had been stowed in Murphy's car, Ted tied the ponies head to tail once more, said good-bye in his quiet way, and jingled off into the scrub. And with him went their last link with the mountains and the still, vast solitude of high places.

They packed themselves into the car and rattled, crashed, and jolted back to the plains and everyday life.

When they reached the Feltons' house, they found Mr. and Mrs. Felton waiting to greet them. Mr. Felton quickly counted heads and said, "There you are, m'dear, not one missing. Isn't that remarkable?"

"Oh," said Mrs. Felton with a deep sigh, "what a relief." But her gratified expression changed to one of dismay when she was shown the two casualties. She became busy at once.

"Bring them both in immediately," she said sternly. And as Mick began to speak, "Yes, naturally I mean the dog, too. I may be strict, but I'm not inhuman." And with this wild statement she disappeared into the kitchen and proceeded to heat water and assemble dressings and bandages. She shook her head and exclaimed in horror as she bathed and bandaged Tess's fingers and Silver's terribly swollen paw, and except to register the fact that they had both been caught in traps, she refused to listen to the story of their adventures. Then, when it was all over, Silver comfortably bestowed and Tess seated in the softest chair, she announced that she was ready to hear. "Act first and talk afterward is what I always say," she declared.

"And that," said Mick, "is why we never allow Mother to handle firearms."

But now that they had her mind on it, they found her a most satisfactory audience. One after another expressions of horror, excitement, and joy chased themselves across her face, and when the story was finished, she leaned across to Tess with shining eyes and said, "I think you were wonderful, really wonderful. And so is that dog. And to think that you were both caught in the same trap; the *same* trap! Isn't that extraordinary, Hugh?"

Mr. Felton, who had been listening with commendable restraint, smiled at his wife. "I am not quite sure which aspect you find extraordinary," he said carefully. "Personally, I find it all remarkable, and I should very much like to be introduced to—ah—Pinkie."

So they fetched Pinkie, and after a long, spellbound look, Mrs. Felton said in quite a small voice, "It must be his personality that's so wonderful. He's not much to look at, is he?"

That night their sleep was fathoms deep, and not one of them woke until Mrs. Felton pulled them out regretfully the following morning.

"I hate to disturb you," she said to Pat and Tess from among the clumps of scarlet roses and purple grapes of the half-made curtains, "but you've got a long journey today, and I think you ought to make a start."

After breakfast they packed up the utility, and by ten o'clock they were ready to leave. The Feltons came out to see them off.

"When do we see you again?" said Mrs. Felton. "I never like saying good-bye until I know. Next summer?"

"They've taken to going to the sea in the summer," said Mick, as if it were an infectious and slightly unsavory disease.

"Oh, but I thought—I mean, Kathleen said she didn't think Jack would be persuaded to go again." Mrs. Felton opened her deep blue eyes very wide, and it was impossible to tell what was going on behind them. She seemed unaware of the odd little silence that closed in around her last words. It was broken by Jack.

"I've changed my mind. If you're talking to Mum on the phone, tell her I'm open to persuasion. I've realized I left some unfinished business down there by the surf."

Simultaneously the faces of Pat and Tess broke into smiles. Pat opened her mouth to speak, but shut it again as Tess's elbow pressed her ribs.

When they had said good-bye and the Feltons still stood watching the cloud of dust settle back on the track, Mrs. Felton said in a puzzled voice, "I never knew Jack intended to go into business, did you, Hugh? I'd have said he was a country boy through and through."

The Steadmans' utility crossed the creek and the green river flats beside it and turned out onto the road for home.

The plains were still hazy with dust whipped up by

the wind, but away to the east and far above, a mauve shadow in the blue sky, was Calca, dreamlike and insubstantial from so far away, but they knew that their clearing would be glittering after the night's frost, the little spring bubbling, and over the treetops the wedge-tails would be hanging motionless in the crisp air.

It was late in the afternoon when the utility, dusty and travel-stained, emerged from the clump of ironbarks and crossed the last long plain to the Pillana homestead. As Tess saw again the familiar paddocks, the sheds and stables, and the rambling house itself, tucked in among the shrubs and trees of the garden, she felt a deep contentment and a sense of peace, greater almost than she had ever known. The quiet, wide-stretching landscape full of the subtle colors of sunset was friendly and welcoming. She knew now that she would always feel at home here, that she was a stranger no longer.